Wisdom *from* *the* Pearl Necklace

Carol Demma Mau

Copyright © 2023 Carol Demma Mau.

All rights reserved. No part of this book may be reproduced, stored, or transmitted by any means—whether auditory, graphic, mechanical, or electronic—without written permission of both publisher and author, except in the case of brief excerpts used in critical articles and reviews. Unauthorized reproduction of any part of this work is illegal and is punishable by law.

ISBN: 979-8-89031-351-5 (sc)
ISBN: 979-8-89031-352-2 (hc)
ISBN: 979-8-89031-353-9 (e)

Because of the dynamic nature of the Internet, any web addresses or links contained in this book may have changed since publication and may no longer be valid. The views expressed in this work are solely those of the author and do not necessarily reflect the views of the publisher, and the publisher hereby disclaims any responsibility for them.

One Galleria Blvd., Suite 1900, Metairie, LA 70001
1-888-421-2397

To Alex and Holly

ACKNOWLEDGMENTS

Thank you for your support: Frank Pundzak, Annette Morgese, Gerilyn Pundzak, Pat Larson, and Deb Sheppard.

For my inspirational support, I would like to thank these people for their wonderful books: Louise Hay; Sylvia Brown; Doreen Virtue; Rosemary Altea; Carolyn Myss; Brian Weiss, MD; Steven D. Farmer; and Wayne Dyer.

Most importantly, I would like to thank Mother/Father God and all of my guides for pushing me on to complete my contract.

PROLOGUE

According to Native American belief, the oak tree is a sign of strength, endurance, helpfulness, and continuity. Some believe that human beings came from the spirits of the trees.

The ancients believed that the oak tree was a sign of faithful love when seen in a vision.

The Oak Tree

I am the spirit of the oak. I keep the tales of the earth in the rings of my years. I have been here for centuries, collecting stories of the earth and her people. I am truth and love. I am part of this world and the inner world. I am the angel of light to many who love the earth and her inhabitants. I bring my spirit alive to those who care. The Native Americans know me as a protector and the goddess of knowledge of the workings of the inner world. They understand that I protect the little spirits of hope who live in the inner world. They know that I am the vehicle in which the little spirits come forth. These spirits work with the human beings to help care for the earth and keep the earth in balance. This balance requires that they work together to care for and protect the air, water, animals, and land that Mother Earth has provided for them. The little spirits were put here to help the human beings; however, the human beings have forgotten their mission. Fear and greed have replaced their once loving attitude toward Earth. The humans started to take too much from the Earth Mother, and because our earth is a loving mother, she gave everything to her children. All she knows is love. She does not understand greed. She does not understand fear. But she has given too much, and now there is no balance. The humans are sorry, but they don't know how to go back. They are lost inside of their personal comforts and cannot see the way out. The little spirits of the inner world understand the problem. They have united and joined forces around the earth in their quest to reach out to the young ones. Their hope is that the young ones will understand the urgency of the problem, be strong, and show the way to their elders. Their desire is to have the earth children come together to release the grip of greed and fear upon themselves and again be free to enjoy the earth's gifts to the fullest!

After much searching, the little spirits have found a small group of young ones to help in their mission. They have asked me to get the attention of these young ones and to send them to the inner world for their lessons in understanding the nature of themselves and the world they live in.

1

From the morning fog, a light green mist arises and forms itself into a beautiful, graceful, long stretch that slowly begins to encircle the grand old oak tree that stands by the ancient creek in the woods where the Anasazi once lived. Swirling, the mist shapes itself into a silky, slinky strand and heads toward the highest branches. Small, pearlescent balls seem to appear out of nowhere and cling to the delicate green strand, giving the impression of a pearl necklace. At that same moment, a beautiful, diaphanous pale-green woman emerges from the oak. With a look of tenderness, she reaches for the strand of pearls as it circles around her neck. She lets the strand run through her fingers, her branches, in a benediction of gratitude. She is elegant in her movements; she is the soul of the tree. When the strand of luminescent beads reaches the top of the tree, its green glow bursts into an extraordinary rainbow of color that quickly swirls downward, heading toward the oak's exposed roots.

"Can you see her?" Excitedly, Trudy pushes the bush lower to give her friend Adele a better look.

Adele pulls her hand away from her mouth and anxiously whispers, "I can't believe what I'm seeing!"

The rainbow-colored band of light reaches the bottom of the tree and pushes itself into one of the oak tree's gnarled old roots, uncovering a small entryway. The woman of the oak looks toward the two girls hiding behind the bush and smiles a welcome. Her branches reach out to them and then point to the entryway.

"Get down!" Trudy pushes hard on Adele's shoulder, and both girls hit the ground, but the lovely Lady of the Oak catches Trudy's stare and beckons her forward. She stands. Adele grabs the back pocket of Trudy's jeans and tries to pull her down. Even though Trudy is much smaller than her companion, she is able to reach back, grab Adele's arm, and pull her up. Trudy's eyes lock into a hypnotic gaze as she stares at the lady. She walks closer to the tree, dragging her reluctant friend along with her. As the two approach the tree, they can see tiny figures in the pearlescent beads. Trudy thinks that they must be fairies or pixies. *But that would be crazy! This whole thing is crazy! How can I be seeing a green lady in a tree?*

The girls stop near the entryway and watch as the end of the rainbow strand makes its final descent past the Lady of the Oak. The lady's body begins to merge with the silky thread; it is an eerie sight yet beautiful to behold. She smiles again at the girls as she starts swirling to become one with the strand. Down she goes, disappearing like a ghost. As the last bit of light enters the passageway, it turns into a womanly hand, and its fingers beckon the girls to follow.

Poof! It is gone! The tree and the surrounding area look as they should at daybreak.

Both girls stand still and stare at the gnarled root, waiting to see what else will happen. Their hearts thump, and they both feel weak in the knees. Trudy lets go of Adele's arm, but just as she is about to speak, something else happens: a striking red fox jumps from the entryway, its coat brushed and as sleek as that of a show dog. She does not look like an animal that lives in the woods. The fox looks up as though she expects to see the girls; she stares at them for a moment and then nonchalantly walks away, never taking her eyes off of the two humans. Trudy and Adele watch the fox disappear into the morning light.

Mystified, Adele looks for a spot to sit down; she finds an old, fallen tree near the creek that fits her needs. She sits down quietly, too overwhelmed to speak. When Trudy told her that she wanted to show her something in the woods, she had never expected to see this. Trudy walks over, sits down next to her best friend, and looks at her for a moment before speaking.

"Well, that was weird, huh?" she says in a voice that is much too casual.

"Weird? That's what you have to say? Weird?"

Adele jumps up and puts both fists on her hips. Facing Trudy and stomping her foot, she then yells at her like a madwoman, "Are you crazy? This is so much more than weird! How can you be so laid back about seeing this? What's going on here? How long have you known about this?" Then, bending over and putting her hands on Trudy's shoulders, she says, "I know you're strange, girl, but what is this all about? You could have at least given me a hint of what to expect! That's what a good friend would have done! Am I right?"

Trudy's eyes fill with tears. She is surprised by Adele's reaction; she hadn't planned on seeing this either. She takes Adele's hands off of her shoulders and holds them in her own. "I don't know what this is about; that's why I wanted you to see it. Please sit back down." Trudy watches her friend angrily sit back down. Trudy feels like crying and thinks that maybe she shouldn't have shared this, but Adele is her best friend, and she thought that Adele would want to know. Maybe she should have kept this mystery to herself and not asked Adele to come this morning.

"Look, I never expected to see this," Trudy tries to explain. "All I saw yesterday was the green fog around the tree. That's what I brought you out here to see, Adele—not this. I didn't know this was going to happen—really."

Both girls sit in quiet concentration for a while.

Adele tries to calm herself. "I'm sorry about yelling at you. I was just feeling scared." Then, after waiting a few moments, she adds, "Why didn't your so-called angel come help us out?" In a bratty, jealous voice, she adds, "You're always talking about her and how important she is to you. Why didn't you just ask her to come?"

Trudy feels misunderstood and dejected. She ignores the last comment as she looks into her friend's big brown eyes and pats her leg. "Really, Adele, I didn't think that we would see anything like this. I saw the green fog yesterday morning when I took Tinker for a walk before school." Then, shaking her head and shrugging her shoulders, she adds, "I didn't think I needed to ask my angel for help. I didn't think we would see anything like this today—I promise."

Trudy looks sad as she stares back at her friend. Then, after a moment, she adds, "I brought you out here because I wanted you to see the green mist. I wanted you to see it because we're always talking and reading about fairies, and this reminded me of some of the stories where the fairies appeared in a soft, strange mist. That's all. I didn't think we'd see all this—that's for sure—and I didn't want to scare you."

Both girls sit quietly for a while in thoughtful reflection. This is something that they both have to mull over before they begin talking again, or they will end up in an argument, and neither girl wants that. They've been friends for way too long and know each other too well.

After about twenty minutes, Adele jumps up, turns to her companion, and squeals, "I've got an idea." She pulls Trudy up. "Let's go tell Maya what we saw; she knows everything about this place. Maybe she can tell us what it was."

Trudy instantly feels better. This is a great idea.

Both girls start to run through the woods toward Grandma Maya's house. Trudy's long strawberry-blonde ponytail swings in rhythm to her quick strides as she tries to keep up with Adele's long, agile movements. They race along the small stream that leads out of the woods and directly to Maya's house.

Trudy thinks that her best friend is beautiful, and she is jealous of the graceful way that Adele moves as she jumps over the rocks and branches in her path. Adele is light on her feet and agile as a cat. *My friend,* Trudy thinks, *is as pretty as any model I have ever seen.*

Trudy is on the small side for a fourteen-year-old. She is small boned and thin, with delicate features. She is the type of girl whom others will label as "cute" her whole life. She is a good athlete and a good student. When it comes to looks, Adele is the complete opposite. She is tall and elegant; her skin is a rich, creamy brown—a mixture of Mexican and African American. She has a muscular, taut body and is the smartest kid in school. The two girls have been friends from the moment they met as babies. They live next door to one another, and their moms are best friends too.

⚜

Maya Norn, known to all of the neighborhood kids as Grandma Maya, owns the woods and the field that runs behind Trudy and Adele's neighborhood. Her family settled there many years ago—"before the takers came," as her Native American grandmother used to say. Her Norwegian grandfather fell in love at first sight with her grandmother and with the land that her family lived on. He built a lovely house for his beautiful Indian princess on that same land, and Maya now lives in that house.

Maya is around eighty years old; no one knows for sure how old she is. She lives in the house alone, except for Henry the cat. She was married once and had a son. Both were lost to war—her husband in the Korean War and her son in Vietnam. She spends her days improving her land by taking care of the trees and the many gardens that surround her house. Everyone in Hazelton knows of her, and most find her charming. There are a few people in town, however, who would like to see Maya sell her land so that they can improve on it by putting up a shopping mall.

⚜

On this warm autumn Saturday, Maya works in her flower garden at the front of her house. She stops when she hears the girls burst through the bushes at the end of the woods and enter the open field to the east of Maya's small cherry orchard. Using her garden rake, she slowly stands and waves as the girls approach. She is a small, strong-looking woman with a broad smile. Her long, thick braids are now completely gray, and although she is up in years, her face is smooth and soft looking.

Adele stops to pull some leaves out of her hair, so Trudy reaches Maya first. Yelling hello, she grabs Maya in a big hug, almost knocking her over. Maya laughs as they hug. "My goodness! What are you two doing out so early?"

Trudy lets go of Maya, and then Adele takes her turn. "We have something to tell you that you won't believe!" Adele is a bit taller than Maya, and she picks her up off the ground when they hug. "We need to ask you about it."

"Well, put me down, darling, and ask."

Maya's old gray cat, Henry, walks over to see what is happening and meows up at Adele.

Adele drops Maya lightly onto the ground, pats Henry on the head, and then helps Maya fix the large-brimmed garden hat that slipped off her head during the hug. Maya takes one hand of each girl as they walk toward her front porch. All three seem to float up the front steps and into the waiting white wicker rocking chairs. Surprisingly, there are three glasses of lemonade waiting on the small, round white table in front of them. Trudy and Adele look at each other and shrug as they smile; they aren't really taken by surprise—something magical always happens when they are around Maya.

Henry jumps up onto the porch railing to lie down, and Maya gets comfortable in her rocker before she takes a slow sip of her lemonade. "Now, girls, tell me why you're so excited."

Both girls start to speak at once, making them impossible to understand.

"Slow down. One at a time, please." Maya rocks in her chair and smiles over at Henry, who is also trying to listen to what the girls are saying.

"You start, Tru," says Adele, pointing to her friend, "and don't leave anything out!" Henry lays his head down on his paws and curls his tail in anticipation.

"Well, I was walking Tinker in the woods yesterday morning, when I noticed a green mist by the stream, where the old oak tree is. I had never seen a green fog before, so I walked toward it. Tinker walked a few steps with me and then sat down, not moving another step. She sat still and just stared at the fog. When she did this, a light shot out of the mist toward the oak tree; it moved slowly and started to swirl around the tree. I watched it for a few seconds, and then I heard my mom yelling for me to come to breakfast. I wanted to stay, but Tinker started pulling on her leash, and you know how big my German shepherd is, so she pulled me back home."

Adele puts down her lemonade. "You told me you saw it on your way to school."

"I did. It was still there when I left for school, but it had disappeared by the time I came home. That's when I went to your house to make a date for this morning."

"We saw more than that this morning," Adele interrupts. "We saw a beautiful green lady appear from the tree. She was very tall and thin. We also saw these little balls of light with tiny people in them; they rode along the strand of light, and then they disappeared into the roots of the tree. It was really weird!" Adele smiles at Trudy.

Henry hisses as he stands and arches his back. He has spotted a fox in the distance and wants to let everyone know that it is there.

"Look, Adele. There's the fox." Trudy stands and walks to the porch rail, where Henry is. She feels that the eyes of the fox are looking right at her. The fox doesn't move; it just stares back, making Trudy feel a bit uneasy.

"We saw that fox jump out of the tree," Adele explains to Maya. "I think it's following us."

The fox turns its head slightly and looks at the old woman sitting with the girls. The woman nods politely to the fox, and the fox nods back and starts to walk away. The girls see the exchange and don't know what to make of it. Henry lies back down and relaxes.

"What day is it today?" Maya asks. She doesn't keep any timepieces or calendars; she feels that they force people to rush to get things done, and she likes to take her time with everything.

"It's Saturday," Adele answers, but she is thinking about the fox and watching her friend, who is still looking out over the porch rail.

"I mean the date," Maya persists.

Trudy turns around and faces Maya. "It's October twenty-eighth," she says in a monotone voice. "You nodded to the fox, and it went away. Why?"

"Did I? Well, I supposed that it had other things to do; after all, it is a creature of the night, and it is well past dawn."

"Why did you want to know the date, Maya?" Adele feels that Maya isn't going to talk about the fox anymore.

Maya smiles at Adele and asks, "Do you know what the fall equinox is?"

Adele answers as if she is in school. "It's the time of year when the sun crosses the equator, making nighttime and daytime the same length." "Yes, that's true. But did you know that it is deemed a magical time of year for many people?"

The girls shake their heads. Trudy sits back down to listen to Maya, but the fox never leaves her thoughts.

"The ancients used to celebrate this time of year with a festival. Many cultures around the world thought that this was an important time, and they regarded the evening of October thirty-first as a time to celebrate the mysteries of the earth."

Adele likes Maya's drawn-out answers. They make her feel relaxed, as if they are playing a game. "Okay, but what has this got to do with what we saw in the woods?"

"Or the fox?" adds Trudy. She has picked up Henry and now has him in her arms.

Maya rocks in her chair as she speaks. "When I was a young girl, my great-grandmother would tell me the story of the Little People. She said that some of the people of the Cherokee Nation could see these Little People in the early hours of the morning around the time of the autumn equinox. The Little People would come out of the wooded areas here on beams of light; she said that they looked like a beautiful pearl necklace floating through the woods, in and around the trees. If you could get close enough, you could see the Little People in the balls of light. They were very hard to see because they moved quickly, and when there were many of them together, they looked like a mist or fog over the waters. She told me that the Little People lived under the earth so that they could take care of all growing things and that during certain times of the year, they would emerge from their homes near the roots of the oak trees to celebrate their work. She said that there were also some that lived under the waters to keep the rivers, lakes, and oceans clean for the water animals." Maya stops and takes a sip of her lemonade, and in her mind, she debates whether or not she should continue with her thoughts. She knows what the girls have seen but isn't sure they will understand the meaning. She takes a long look at their faces and decides to continue. "I believed that my great-grandmother was talking about the same kind of Little People that the Celts and other cultures talked about: the fairies. So as a child, I would always go looking for the lights in the woods—the Little People in the pearl necklace—especially during this time of year. Once, just once, I saw them by that same oak tree next to the creek."

"The same tree?" Both girls are excited.

"Yes, I believe so. I did not see the beautiful woman that you spoke about, but I did see some Little People gliding down a soft green-looking mist. Their small bodies were riding along a strand of light in what I thought were tiny bubbles, and it did look like a pearl necklace. They rode straight down into the root of the tree as the green mist turned into a lovely rainbow of colored light. I remember how excited I was as I watched that most enchanting sight. They were so tiny. I also remember that I could hear some music; it was strange and a bit hypnotic …" Maya's voice trails off. She stares straight ahead with a dreamy look.

Trudy doesn't want to interrupt Maya's remembrances, but she can't help herself. "Did you see the fox too?"

"The fox?" It takes a moment for Maya to come out of her trance. "Oh, the fox. No. But I can tell you that the fox is an animal of the between times. Its powers of magic come during dusk and dawn, and if you see it during these times, it can be a guide into the realm of the Little People. My people believe that the fox is a shape-shifter with magic in the feminine energies. It is a very powerful totem."

Neither girl asks Maya what a totem is; they just assume Maya will eventually tell them, so they wait. No answer comes, nor does the question.

The three sit rocking in silence for a while before finishing their lemonade. Maya reminisces about her encounter as a young girl. Adele thinks about what happened earlier that day. Trudy gazes out across the fields around Maya's house while she scratches Henry behind the ears; she is looking for the elusive fox. She knows in her heart that the fox came for her. What she doesn't know is why.

Trudy lies in her bed, unable to sleep, staring at the ceiling. All she can think about is tomorrow and what might happen. After their meeting with Maya, Adele agreed to meet with Trudy at dawn, and the two of them will go back to the oak tree to try to figure out what is going on out there in the woods. Trudy hopes that they will see the Little People, the lady, and the fox. It is exciting to think about. Would it be like the movies? Would they be friendly? Would they be like the storybook fairies that hide away from humans and play jokes on them? Would they try to catch one? Could they talk to them? All these questions keep going around in her head, making sleep impossible.

While Trudy's mind is busy conjuring up more questions and ideas, her eyes begin to focus on the soft pink-and-white ball of light that has quietly entered her room. She is used to seeing this shimmering soccer-ball-sized light. She knows it is her guardian angel. It moves slowly around her room before stopping a few feet from Trudy's face. Trudy always feels a warm calm when the ball of light appears; it is never frightening. She can't remember a time when the ball of light wasn't around; she sees it almost every night. Sometimes it moves close enough for her to see the beautiful face of the angel inside of it. It was Maya who told her it is a guardian angel and explained how lucky she is to be able to see it, because most people cannot. There are times when

Trudy thinks that she can hear the angel talking to her, but the words just come into her thoughts; she really doesn't hear anything. The angel always tells her that she is a precious child and that she is deeply loved; it is comforting. Trudy is always happy to see the ball of light.

"Precious child," the angel whispers into Trudy's thoughts. "I am always with you. I will be with you tomorrow, so remember to call upon me if you should need my help. I cannot interfere if you don't ask for me; it is the way that the universe works."

Trudy is surprised to hear this and sits up in bed. "Did you hear what I was thinking about?" This is the first time Trudy has ever tried to talk with her angel, and she finds that it excites her.

The sweet, soft voice penetrates her thoughts, and she hears an answer: "I can always hear you," it says, "but I cannot always come between you and what is happening to you unless I am asked. My job is to protect you when you want me to, but I cannot interfere with your life lessons unless it is to help make them a bit easier for you to handle. Do you understand?"

"Yes, I think so."

Trudy sees the face in the light smile, and then the ball starts to move upward.

"Stop!" Trudy says out loud. "What is your name?"

"What would you like to call me?"

Trudy thinks for a minute; she tries to think of the most beautiful name she can. "Danielle!" It is her favorite aunt's name.

"Danielle—then that is my name." The glowing pink orb moves upward and starts shrinking. It gets smaller and smaller until the angel disappears into a tiny burst of twinkling lights that fades quickly.

Trudy lies in bed smiling; she feels wonderful and loved. It is the best feeling ever. She then quickly falls into a deep and peaceful slumber, dreaming of the beautiful pearl necklace.

It is still dark when Trudy meets Adele at the end of her driveway. The path to the woods starts behind the Truhardts' garage. They walk silently to the back of the garage, jump the old wire fence, and start down the hardened mud trail that leads to the oak tree.

Adele throws her arm out to halt Trudy. "Look, Tru—someone's fishing at the creek, right behind the tree. It looks like Jeff."

Trudy sees Jeff, and she also sees Richie with his fishing rod perched over the water's edge.

"Hi, guys!" A small voice rings out.

Adele and Trudy both jump in fright. They turn around to see Richie's little brother, Doni, standing there with all of his fishing gear.

"What are you guys doin' out here so early? You gonna fish with us?" Doni keeps walking toward his brother and Jeff.

Trudy and Adele sigh deeply; they are disappointed that they have to deal with these three. It's not because they don't like them; they just prefer to keep this adventure to themselves.

"No, we're not out here to fish," answers Adele. "We're just taking a walk."

"Well, hi, ladies. How are you this fine morning?" Jeff waves a greeting to the girls and then adjusts his cap to fit over his short Afro. Richie just waves. He is shy around girls. Even though he and Jeff are both fourteen, Richie looks younger. Jeff is tall and thin, wears glasses, and has a fine dark brown complexion that frames his handsome face. Richie has that surfer-boy look, with long blond hair and hazel eyes. The girls think his shyness makes him cute; however, Richie never notices. Doni doesn't look like his older brother at all. Doni has brown hair and is tall for a nine-year-old, almost as tall as his brother. The only feature that they have in common is the hazel color of their eyes.

"We're fine." Adele smiles at Jeff and keeps walking toward the tree. Both girls are looking for the green mist or the light that it produces.

"Strange to see you girls out here walking this early in the morning." Jeff addresses the girls but keeps his eye on his fishing line.

"No stranger than us seeing you," Adele snaps back. She likes kidding around with Jeff.

Trudy walks around to the other side of the giant oak. She tries to find the root that she saw the light enter the day before. She gets down on her knees and starts to brush some of the leaves away.

"Whatcha doin'?" Doni has followed Trudy and is standing right behind her.

"Looking for something I saw here yesterday," she says as she moves from root to root, brushing away the leaves and trying to ignore Doni. All of a sudden, Trudy feels a pull on her hand, sort of like a vacuum. She stops and looks at where her hand is lying; there is a slight green mist coming out from the area where she is feeling the vacuum. "Look, Doni. Look!"

Doni drops his fishing gear, gets down on his hands and knees, and crawls to where Trudy has her hand. "What's that green stuff?"

"Put your hand here." Trudy grabs Doni's hand and puts it in the mist so that he can feel the pull. The mist moves over their hands and starts forming itself into a strand of green light that is now beginning to encircle the tree.

Doni feels the vacuum and looks down at his hand. "Trudy! My hand is shrinking!" He yanks his hand up and out of Trudy's hold, causing both of them to tumble backward. They look at each other and then back at the gnarled root.

The others have heard the outburst and come running.

"What happened?" Adele gets down on her knees to check Trudy and Doni. "Are you all right?" Jeff and Richie kneel down; Richie brushes the top of his brother's head with his hand to make sure he is okay.

Saying nothing, both Trudy and Doni point toward the green mist. Then Trudy starts crawling back toward it. She puts her index finger in front of her lips to silence them and then points again at the opening.

Everyone stops and stares; in the mist is a tiny, glittery ball of light moving around. They all get down on their stomachs and wiggle closer.

The ball of light stops moving but continues to twinkle. There is a tiny being in the light. Everyone sees it; the little being looks back at them and waves. The watchers are astonished; they look around at each other and then back at the little being.

"Is she a fairy?" Doni whispers.

No one speaks, but the little ball of light jumps quickly up and down as if to answer yes, and then the fairy waves at them again. She is dressed in a green-and-brown outfit of leaves that matches the surrounding area well. She has reddish-brown hair and lovely, glittery, shiny wings that move so quickly that they can barely make them out. She looks as though she is waving at them to follow her into the entryway, into the mist. Her smile is welcoming and sweet.

"She wants us to follow her," says Trudy.

"How can we follow her? She can see that we're way too big. What should we do?" Adele feels silly even suggesting that they follow the little being. This is crazy.

"Let's catch her," Jeff proposes. "I'll get one of my bait jars."

"No!" yells Richie, startling everyone. He slaps his hand onto Jeff's back to hold him down.

Richie's loud voice causes the shimmering orb to zoom quickly upward; the rapid movement makes everyone gasp out loud.

"You're scaring her away!" Doni cries.

"Look, there she is!" Trudy points. "Near the middle of the tree. See?"

Cautiously, the orb descends. No one else dares to move; they keep their eyes glued to her.

"Do you hear music?" Adele barely murmurs the words.

Richie looks at her and nods.

"Sounds kind of like a flute." Jeff speaks as quietly as he can.

As the fairy reaches the gnarled opening in the root of the old oak, a bright cone of crystal light appears. It shoots out of the entryway and gets larger as it ascends into the sky. The green mist encircles it at the bottom, giving it an eerie look. The little person stops there, waves to the group to follow her, and then darts under the gnarled root and vanishes. The music lingers a moment longer, and then it is gone too.

"Wow! That was awesome!" Jeff cries out. "But I think we should have tried to catch her."

"Well, I have a better idea—let's follow her," Trudy commands.

Everyone turns to look at Trudy. They are startled by the directness of her outburst. It is so unlike Trudy.

"Well?" she challenges.

No one moves or says a word; they just continue to gaze at Trudy. Everyone is still in shock over what they have just seen and heard.

Trudy walks over to the cone of light; the vacuum pull now feels much stronger than before. She slowly puts her hand into it. To her amazement, and everyone else's, her hand starts to shrink down. Then her arm shrinks as it is pulled into the cone. Adele clutches Trudy's other hand and smiles at her; she is ready to go too. Doni takes Adele's free hand and grabs his brother's hand as well. Jeff then takes Richie's left hand so that they are all linked together and ready to embrace their next move.

Trudy gives in to the vacuum; she experiences a tingling sensation as she shrinks down and is drawn into the opening. The others watch as Trudy's body becomes smaller and smaller and moves toward the entryway. Adele is quickly pulled in after her, as are the rest of them.

It's like flying, Trudy thinks. It feels wonderful to float into this beautiful rainbow-colored light. She looks back to see who has followed and is pleased to see that everyone has come along. The vacuum gets stronger as they enter the passageway under the gnarled root. She notices that they aren't going straight down but are moving along in a slight decline, a small tunnel. She can see the underground roots of the tree and smell the earth as she moves. The biggest surprise is that it isn't dark; it is like twilight. She can see the end of the tunnel, and as she stares toward it, she also sees the red tail of a fox as it slips through the opening. Trudy turns to see if Adele has seen it too and realizes that she has as soon as they make eye contact. However, neither of them says a word about it; they are both enjoying this strange little trip and don't want to break the spell that they are moving under.

They begin to slow down as they reach the opening, and their feet drop to the ground. They are all still holding hands when the vacuum dies down. They walks out of the tunnel together, and what they see takes their breath away.

When the group exits the tunnel, they are a bit bewildered by the sight. The colors surrounding them are much brighter than anything they have seen before. The smell of the air is glorious; it is fresh and clean and crystal clear. Every blade of grass, every leaf, and every flower are perfect, except that they are much larger than they should be.

"Look how big everything is!" Doni looks around in wonderment. "The grass is taller than me!"

"This is fantastic!" exclaims Adele.

They slowly let go of each other's hands and venture out around the area near the tunnel, walking on a lush carpet of emerald-green moss.

"Listen," Richie says. "Do you hear the music?"

Everyone stops to listen.

"Barely," Adele answers. "It seems to be all around us. Doesn't it?"

"Look," Trudy interrupts. She is pointing at a large rock by the tunnel. "Doesn't this look like writing?" She wipes the stone where she sees the engravings, and she tries to make sense of the words. "But I can't read it."

"It's elemental graphology," a soft, musical voice answers.

Trudy jumps and quickly turns around; she is startled by the unfamiliar voice. Behind her is the fairy that they followed; she is much larger now but still a lot smaller than Trudy. Her features are fine and dainty; she moves gracefully about and has a lovely smile that contains a bit of mischief. Everyone stares in awe.

"It says that this is the entrance to the outer world. That is where you just came from," the fairy explains. She then flies over to another rock. "And this one says, 'Welcome to the Otherworld of Earth.' The otherworld is here where I live." She smiles and moves about as she speaks. "My name is Lilly, and I am one of the daughters of Dancing Waters, queen of this region. I am here to welcome you and show you about." She does a small curtsy. "Please follow me; I would like the others to know that you are here."

"Wait. Wait!" Jeff throws his arms up in a gesture indicating for her to stop and then points to the rock. "Why does this say '*Entry* to the Outer World,' when the vacuum pulled us through it and we exited out of the tunnel? Shouldn't it say *exit*?"

The fairy smiles at Jeff and then flies over to the rock. "For us, it is an entryway; however, we can use it for both. It just depends which way you are going. If you enter here"—she points at the tunnel—"it will take you back."

Jeff walks over to where she is pointing and notices that there are two paths. As he approaches the tunnel to examine the paths, two large dragonflies and a damselfly come darting out of it, causing him to duck so that he won't be knocked over. "Whoa!" he yells. "What was that?"

"Dragonflies," Lilly answers. "The blue one was a damselfly."

"They were giant!" Jeff readjusts his glasses. "Where did they come from?"

"The tunnel, of course." The fairy is puzzled by his question. Didn't he just see them fly out? Then she understands what he meant. "It is natural for animals, reptiles, and some insects to use the passageways; they go back and forth all the time, bringing us news of the outer world. They are our messengers and friends."

Trudy is fascinated. "You mean that there is more than this one passageway to the other world?"

"Oh yes. There are many passageways into our world. The ancients used them all the time; that's why there are so many tales about all of us." The fairy giggles.

Doni walks up to Lilly. "You said all animals and reptiles but only some insects. Why?"

"Because there are some insects that plague the earth and do not belong here in this place; they were conjured up as destroyers, and since we are the preservers of Earth, they are not allowed here. They do not help themselves or others, nor do they have any reasoning, deduction, or memory. They cannot see the passageways; therefore, they do not enter. Your outer world believes that all insects and arachnids have little or no thinking power, but that is only true with some. The helpful ones have instincts like animals; of course, they are not as strong, but they are there nonetheless. The spiders are the most intelligent, and some of them are our most celebrated storytellers. They have passed the stories of the earth down through all time, using their webs to keep the histories. I will be happy to show you one if you'd like." Lilly then waves for the children to follow her.

Adele grabs Trudy's arm. "Wait!" she yells. "Maybe we should go back. Maybe we should go home."

Trudy turns to her friend. "What's wrong?"

"I'm afraid we won't find our way back home. I don't want to stay here!" She starts to cry.

Lilly flies over to Adele and touches her cheek. "My dear, don't worry. I promise you that you will get back home. We don't want to harm any of you or make you feel bad. Our intentions are pure. It is important for us to show our visitors our world. We want you to understand how wonderful the earth truly is and see the great things she has to share with all of her inhabitants. If you want to go back now, you can; however, I invite you to stay for a while and see this earthly paradise in which we live."

Adele feels the fairy's light touch upon her face and is immediately comforted. She no longer is afraid and decides she will stay with her friends for a short while.

The fairy flies to the front of the group. "Come—let me show you around a bit. I think that you will like what you see. Follow me." Lilly flies up a little higher than the heads of her followers so that they all can see her. Everyone keeps up with her as she leads them through the foliage that is around the entryway; the tall grass magically parts for them as they move forward. The mossy ground is like a carpet, and the enormous daisies sway and seem to bow as they walk past them. Everything is huge but beautiful, and the fragrance of all the flowers is extraordinarily pleasing.

They walk across a small pond with stepping stones, and as they reach the other side, Trudy thinks she sees the fox rushing through the tall grass. She turns to Adele. "Did you see it?" She points to where she saw the fox.

"What?"

"The fox—I saw the fox, Adele. It followed us here."

"Maybe it's not the same fox. Just forget about it, Tru. You scare me when you get fixated on something."

Trudy feels unsettled, but she will try to do what her friend asked. Maybe it was another fox. *And maybe it wasn't.*

Lilly continues to talk as they walk. "There are so many fantastic things that the earth has to offer each one of us. Humans used to understand, but they have forgotten. Humans need to remember how to work in harmony with our planet in order to survive. In losing that memory of survival, they have also lost the ability to see us. That is why our world has become so secret. That is why most cannot see us."

"I don't understand," says Jeff. "I think that our scientists and researchers are doing a great job in trying to do the right things on our planet. Every day, they discover new health treatments for our people and our planet."

"You are right about that; however, many of the health problems that you are talking about wouldn't be a problem at all if we had continued to work together the way that we did a long time ago. Humans have put too much belief into technology and not enough into themselves. Belief that technology will always be the way out has become the norm, but humans need to start believing in themselves again. We all need to believe in the strength of each other and ourselves. We need to stop hurting each other with our actions and our words and start helping. Humans need to learn to love themselves again." Lilly stops preaching; she sees in their faces that they do not understand her the way that she intended. "I'm sorry. I didn't mean to be preachy. I want you to have a wonderful visit with us and see the world in which I live with love."

Everyone walks together, a healthy curiosity in every heart. They are excited to be with the bewitching and charming little Lilly. The graceful way that she moves is enticing; however, it is the exquisite landscape that dazzles this group and makes them want to continue on their glorious adventure.

While Trudy walks along the soft, mossy path, her thoughts turn to Maya. She wishes that Maya could be with them and see this fascinating wonderland. She also thinks about all the books that she has read about fairies and the faraway places that they are supposed to live in, and she wonders how many Americans know that this place exists. She feels happy to be a part of this expedition.

Adele is a bit more cautious in her thinking. She is mindful of every detail. She is going to remember every step that they take so that she can get back home.

Doni, on the other hand, is excited. He thinks that maybe they will get a chance to meet the great Peter Pan and the Lost Boys, and the idea of maybe fighting pirates arouses his imagination.

Richie is in quiet contemplation; he is watchful of his surroundings and expects the unusual at every turn. He pulls out his pencil and a pad of paper from his back pocket and tries to write down everything that has happened to them thus far on this crazy journey.

Jeff is fearless in his movements. He, like Trudy, is happy and excited to be here, but he also feels some responsibility in keeping everyone safe.

Lilly leads her troop past an immense birch tree; its outspread branches are so beautifully entwined that they look like a threesome of angels swaying in a hypnotic dance. As Trudy gazes upon this glorious sight, she can feel her own angel around her, giving her a clear sense of respect for all of nature and its circle of constant change. *Nature is always involved in a dance of change.* Trudy is in deep thought, and when she looks up to see which way Lilly is leading them, she is surprised to see Lilly looking right back at her. They make eye contact, and Lilly winks and smiles as if she knows exactly what Trudy is thinking. This gesture makes Trudy feel warm inside. She feels a connection to everything. All is complete but moving and changing at the same time. It is a perfect symphony of feeling.

"Look, here's one!" Lilly is excited as she points to an enormous spiderweb that is connected to the stalk of a sunflower and its outstretched leaves. Everyone looks up at this extraordinary sight. There before them is an entire field of giant sunflowers with webs. The silken threads of the webs are lightly dripping with dew. The sun is shining upon them, making each web sparkle with a glittery rainbow effect. The sight is so dazzling that the group lets out an "Ooh" when they see it.

Jeff is admiring the beauty, as everyone else is; however, his instinctive approach to the ways of nature has him also looking for the weaver of these giant webs.

Lilly picks up on Jeff's thoughts. "Oh, don't worry—the makers of these webs have long gone, Jeff. The spiders spin their webs and then move on to tell the history of another. The spiders are hard workers, they never sit still, and in this world, they will not hurt you." Lilly flies to the middle of a web and looks down upon Jeff as if anticipating his next question. "My wings will not be caught in this web—it is not like the webs in your world—and our creatures do not eat one another. These webs keep the history, or story, of a being or an event; sometimes both are told in one web."

"How do you read the story?" Doni is totally enthralled.

"Watch." Lilly slides along the silken threads as if she is ice skating, only slower, her hands and feet lightly touching the threads as she moves. A soft, musical sound rises from the web as she sweeps along; it is like the musical sound that rises from a crystal glass when one lightly rubs his or her wet finger around the rim. She is smiling, and her eyes are closed. "This is the life of a poor but happy child that grows to tell many stories that brighten and lighten the burdens of others. He is a funny adult; he makes people laugh at themselves. He has many problems to overcome, but he does so joyously. He is not a complainer. Others see him as having an easy life; however, he has had to learn his life lessons like everyone else. He keeps his heartaches to himself and eventually learns to give them up to the universal All. He departs this lifetime as a very old man who was much loved by the world." Lilly stops and turns to the onlookers; she has a big smile on her face. "This is a beautiful life story!"

"Who is it?" Richie asks.

"It is the story of one's life that is important, not the name."

"But people want to be remembered!" Adele cries out softly.

"He is remembered through his life story. Many will know him from this remembrance, but more will keep him in their hearts by telling and retelling his funny stories to their children, and they too will pass them on. Many people benefit from the lessons he has learned in this lifetime. Everyone benefits in some way from another's life. We are all connected." Lilly can see from their faces that she is not relating to the group the way that she wants to. "Come—I'll introduce you to some of the other Earth elementals that I live with."

Lilly is once again leading the way through the giant plants. The group can still hear the music that they heard when they first arrived. It hasn't gotten any louder, nor has it gotten any softer. It just is. It adds to the beauty of the land.

Trudy is eager find out where the fairy is leading them and is ready to ask about their journey, when she feels something lightly touch her arm. When she turns to look at who is trying to get her attention, she hears a small giggle. Then Richie thinks he feels something touch the ball cap he has rolled up in his back pocket with his notepad, but when he reaches to swat it away, there is nothing there. Then there is a burst of many amused giggles. Everyone starts looking around to see where the noise might be coming from. An unexpected whoosh of wind startles them, and then, magically, a half dozen fairies float out in front of them, smiling and laughing. They have long and short hair; blond, brown, red, and black hair; curly and straight hair. They are different shapes and different colors, but they are all divinely beautiful.

Lilly is excited to see all of them. The fairies hug each other in greeting and then fly around and in between the visitors, saying hello and welcome. It is a glorious sight to behold; everyone stands smiling, stunned at what they are seeing.

"The damselfly told us you were coming," announces a dark brown fairy with long, curly hair. "We were too excited to wait, and we just had to come out to greet you!" The fairy puts both of her hands to her lips and then throws a kiss to the group.

"Welcome! Welcome! Welcome!" The smallest fairy sings out these words. He is cute, with short blond hair and quick movements that make everyone laugh.

"You're right," says the red-haired fairy to Lilly. "The laughter of humans is the most wonderful sound on Earth!"

Another fairy, one with shoulder-length black curls and dark brown skin, flies up to Adele. "We're so happy that you decided to stay!" Then, pulling on Adele's shirt collar, she yells, "Come on. Hurry! We're going to have a party!"

"A party!" yells Doni. "Let's go!"

"Okay, just follow me," says the small blond imp to Doni. "We'll have a great time!"

Everyone follows Lilly and the fairy group; they look as if they are heading toward a huge oak tree that has appeared in the distance. As they walk, Jeff wonders how this can be happening. *How could that gigantic tree be here and not be seen on the other side? How could all of this be here?*

As they approach the outstretched shadows of the oak tree's branches, they see a golden light surrounding the trunk of the tree. The grasses around it are moving as if a great crowd is gathering there, but they can see no one. The group grasps each other's hands in happy anticipation. They are thrilled to be with these fun-loving creatures and can't wait to see what will happen next.

Doni suddenly stops. His sudden halt causes the whole group to pull up on one another and bump into each other.

"Look at that!" he yells.

Up ahead and to the right side of this gleeful little party is an enormous turtle with a couple of passengers riding on its back. The passengers are sitting on a blanket, and the figure in front is holding reins attached to a bridle that is in the turtle's mouth. When the riders hear Doni yell out, they turn to look in his direction.

"Hi, Ansel!" Some of the fairies fly toward the turtle, waving. "Hi, Darla! Hi, Sam!"

The small blond fairy pats the turtle's head. "Hi, Milo!"

"Are these our party guests?" Ansel asks the fairies. Ansel has no wings, nor do the others who ride with him.

"Why, yes—yes, they are," Lilly answers proudly as the leader of the group.

"Well, introduce us then." Ansel stands up on the back of the waiting turtle; he is thin and has a large nose and a small face.

Lilly pauses and takes a moment to look at her group. She flies to Trudy, first introducing her and then each of the others in turn, giving Ansel their names.

Ansel bows slightly and introduces himself and his family. "I am Ansel, and we are pixies from the mist by the creek called Crabapple." Next, sweeping his hand toward the female, he says, "This is my life companion, Darla." Then, stooping a bit, he adds, "And this is our son, Sam." He then walks over to the front of the turtle and says, "This lovely beast is Milo." Milo nods hello.

Ansel walks back and again addresses the group. "We are pleased that you've come for a visit. We always enjoy a chance to party." He has a huge grin on his face.

Darla stands up, brushes off her brightly colored dress, and, in a sweet voice, says, "I love to get dressed up and welcome visitors. We haven't had many lately, but our visitor parties are the best!"

Sam tugs at his mother's skirt. "Let's go. I want to see my friends."

"Oh dear, don't be rude, Sam. Stand up and say hello."

The smallest pixie stands and politely bows; he has an anxious smile mixed with a bit of mischief. "Hi," he says quickly. "Welcome." He turns and looks at his father and gives him a look that says, *Let's go.*

"Well, we'll be getting along now." Ansel and his family sit back down. "We'll see you there!" They all wave good-bye, and Milo nods as they start back down the pathway.

Adele leans into Trudy and whispers, "This is all so strange. Isn't it?" Both girls giggle.

"Yeah, I can't wait to see what happens next," Trudy whispers back.

Immediately after Trudy says this, the girls hear a little laugh, and one of the fairies says, "We have very good hearing," and then they hear a few more giggles.

"Oh, I didn't mean anything bad," Adele says sheepishly. "I just think this is so different than where I come from. That's all."

"Come on—let's get to the party!" says Doni anxiously.

Everyone laughs at Doni's little outburst.

Richie pulls out his small pad and pencil. "Maybe you could tell us your names before we get there. I want to remember all of you."

Jeff walks over, looks down at Richie's pad, and sees that he has been taking notes. "What are you going to do with that? Write a book?"

"Naw, I just want to remember everything."

"You think you're going to forget this?"

Lilly flies up to Jeff. "You'd be surprised how many visitors go back to the outer world and convince themselves that this world is not really here. We welcome the idea that Richie wants to remember us.

"I'll be happy to introduce everyone to all of you." Lilly touches the fairy next to her on the shoulder. "This is Orange Blossom; we just call her Blossom." Orange Blossom smiles and waves, her black curls bouncing. Her skin is a soft dark brown. She wears an orange dress that looks like a tutu, and she has orange blossoms in her hair.

Lilly goes to the smallest fairy next. "This is Timothy, but we all call him Topsy."

Topsy says a quick, high-pitched hello and then darts out of the way.

The red-haired fairy is sitting on Richie's shoulder, reading off of his cnotepad. She has straight, long, flowing hair and the most beautiful full-lipped smile. "My name is Margaret; my friends call me Maggie," she tells him, and then she points to the fairy floating beside her, who is just a little bit rounder than the rest of them. She has the face of a true Mexican beauty. "This is Magdalena."

Magdalena pushes her long dark brown hair aside. "Welcome. I'm so happy to meet you!"

The last two fairies are twins; they are taller than the others and are boys. They have straight black hair that matches their Asian appearance and are kind of tough looking for fairies, but both have great smiles and are nice.

"This is Will and Phil," announces Lilly. "We've been friends for a very long time and have had many wonderful adventures together." She flies up to both of them and kisses each one of them on the cheek. Will and Phil both blush a bit and then bow to the group in welcome.

"We're very happy to meet all of you," says Trudy, smiling. "Thanks for the introductions, but I do have a question that I need to ask, if that's okay?" Seeing that the fairies are waiting for her to continue, she presses on. "I was wondering why you are living here—I mean this in the nicest way, of course. I thought that fairies were only in certain parts of the world, like Ireland. I've never really thought that you actually lived here in the United States."

Lilly is eager to answer this question. "We are everywhere on the earth. We are called different names in other countries, and we look a little different as you travel from place to place, but we are everywhere that there are humans. We are always around."

Everyone is a bit surprised to hear this.

Topsy flies around everyone, waving his arms in a gesture to get them moving and on their way. His glossy, see-through rainbow-colored wings are moving so quickly that they can barely see them. "Come on!" his small voice squeaks. He is excited.

"Yes, yes. Come on!" Magdalena is also in a hurry to get the group moving.

All the fairies then try to push the group along. They are talking quickly and in high-pitched voices—so high that at times, they are hard to understand.

Everyone gets the idea, and taking hands, they start to move toward the golden glow arising from the great oak that has appeared before them.

6

The background music gets louder as they approach the golden glow of the giant oak tree. The tall grasses become much shorter as they reach the end of the path, and they can see a great number of guests arriving.

"Look!" Adele leans into Trudy and whispers as she points ahead. Before them, they can see many different types of fairies, pixies, and elves heading for an opening at the base of the oak tree. "This is so exciting! Aren't they cute?" Some of them are tall, and others are very small, while some others look a bit strange.

"Is that a mermaid with wings?" asks Doni to no one in particular.

Blossom answers, "Yes, she is a water nymph, or sprite. Isn't she beautiful?"

The sprite turns her head toward Doni and throws him a kiss; her long blonde ringlets bounce a little as she also waves her shiny blue-green tailfin at them and then flies off on her way to the party.

The crowd thickens as they near the entrance. The tree is as tall as a skyscraper, its roots stretching out like giant, gnarled fingers. Trudy notices that the noise that surrounds them sounds more like a swarm of insects than the flock-of-geese sound that humans make when there are many of them gathered together. It is a good sound that reminds her of Maya's gardens.

The entrance is crowded; the two large, picturesque doors are pressed back against the tree as far as they can go. There are lifelike carvings of beautiful faces on each door, every face giving a welcoming smile to all who enter. Everyone smiles and waves to the human visitors; it is exciting to be the main attraction in this endless sea of fairy people.

Passing through the doors, they can now see the great hall. Everything is bathed in a glorious, twinkling golden light. There is a wonderful, sweet smell, like the best kind of candy. The room is packed, but there is no pushing or shoving. Everyone is smiling as the crowd moves slowly into the great hall, taking care not to knock over any of the beautiful decorations of wildflowers and garden roses that adorn it.

Trudy can see the tops of two golden thrones as she descends the stairway, and as she gets closer, she can see that they are connected and are carved from the stump of one tree.

"Wow. Just look at this place—it's amazing." Jeff can't help but blurt this out. "I can't believe this is all here."

Adele puts her hand on Jeff's back and agrees. "Isn't it the most beautiful place you've ever seen?"

"It makes me want to have some candy." Doni licks his lips as he says this.

Next to Doni is a gnome who is almost his height. "You're smelling the best chocolate in the universe, and we make it right here on good old Mother Earth. The smell is glorious, isn't it?"

Doni looks down at the gnome, who is smiling up at him. "But I smell more than chocolate; there are all kinds of delicious smells here."

The gnome nods his approval of Doni's sense of smell and smiles back as he moves on in to the enchanted hall.

Jeff and Richie start to lag behind—Jeff because he is trying to memorize everything he sees, and Richie because he is writing everything down. As Richie quickly scribbles down his impressions, he feels a light tap on his left shoulder. When he glances up, he sees a small angel next to him. The apparition is an opaque dark brown, with black hair and beautiful, large light brown feathered wings. When Richie looks at him, he has the feeling that he has known this being for a long time.

Richie stops walking and turns to look at this being head-on. "Who are you?"

"I'm Jamie, your muse," the small angel-like creature announces.

"My what?" says Richie. The muse has flown forward and is right in front of his face, smiling at him.

Jamie bows slightly. "Your muse," he says. "I help you with your writing."

"I've never seen you before. What is a muse, and how do you help me?" Richie feels that this small being is joking with him.

The muse points his finger at Richie and uses a more serious tone when he speaks. "Now, that is an important question." He then proceeds to sit in an imaginary chair before he continues. "I wish more people would ask about us, but the truth is that most people don't even know we exist. They talk about fairies, gnomes, pixies, angels, mermaids, and even dragons and giants, but alas, few talk about us. We are a mix of fairy and angel; we're a hybrid of sorts. We were created to be of help to writers, musicians, and artists of all kinds; we help them stay on track with their mission. At least, we try to keep them on track, but most ignore our encouragements and help, feeling that we are just a random thought. However, those that listen do very well."

Richie just stares back at the muse for a second before talking again. "I don't remember ever hearing you talk to me before."

The muse starts to dart back and forth in front of Richie; he is agitated by what Richie has just said but is trying to keep his cool. "When you're searching for the perfect word to express your ideas or you magically get a creative thought, it comes from me. I plant the thought in your thinking. I've given you many great ideas that you've just not used." Jamie then slows down and adds, "And a few that you have used as well."

"Aha—come on!" Richie lightly swats at the muse to push him aside and then starts to walk away; he doesn't believe what Jamie is telling him, and he feels that if it were true, it would be an invasion of his private thoughts.

"Richie!" Jamie follows him. "Stop. Please." He pleads, "I can't read your mind; I'm just a planter of ideas. I can't make you do anything you don't want to do, and I can't help you if you don't want the help. I'm your friend."

Richie stops. "Are you telling me that I don't have any creative ideas of my own?"

"Well, no." Jamie hangs his head. "I was bragging a little bit."

Jeff has been watching this whole scene unfold and decides to enter into the discussion. "You mean that you work with Richie in creating thoughts to help him with his writing?"

Jamie flies over to Jeff. "Yes," he says excitedly, "I see a creative thought emerging from Richie, and I encourage it to grow, and if Richie works with me, we can create a wonderful story! But sometimes the thought comes and Richie will just let it pass as a nice thought, and then I can't do much except to let it go too."

Jamie flies back to Richie and smiles. "I just help your ideas and thoughts grow. That's all."

Richie can't resist the muse and smiles back. "Okay, I get it."

At that same moment, a blast of trumpet music comes from inside the great hall. The group stops walking, as does the rest of the crowd.

Lilly turns and whispers to the group, "It's the queen and king!" She points toward the double throne.

From the left side of the great hall, two figures appear. The queen has on a golden gossamer gown with dewdrops all over it that shine like diamonds. It hangs loosely from her shoulders in the Native American fashion. She is wearing a tall crown with uneven points that looks like the bark of a tree except for its golden glow. She has beautiful, long, thick dark braids that hang down past her tiny waist. She is definitely

Native American. The king is holding up her right hand as they walk. He has his black hair in braids that come down to his midback; they are not as long as the queen's. His serious face is handsome and gentle looking. He wears a traditional Native American chieftain's headdress of feathers, a fringed vest, and chaps. The vest and chaps look as if they are made of leather, but they are made of pounded soft bark. Neither of the royal couple wears any shoes.

The queen turns her head to look in the direction of the visiting party and smiles at them. Her smile is glorious; it makes Trudy's stomach feel warm inside. Trudy smiles back at the queen, and the queen nods her approval. The crowd is silent as the royal couple walks to their thrones. No one moves. When the majestic pair finally stands in front of the thrones, the king lets go of the queen's hand and raises both of his hands over his head in a greeting to the throng of guests standing before him. A tremendous roar of happy greetings floods back to him from the crowd, and the gentle background music starts up again. The king and queen both sit down and look directly toward the visitors. The king has just a hint of a smile on his face, but the queen's face is lit with an impressive smile that shows her kindness and goodwill. The queen's stare makes Trudy feel like running up to her to give her a hug, and she can tell by looking at her companions that they feel the same way.

"Come." Lilly gestures to the group. "They want to meet you."

"Go. Go." Jeff pushes on Trudy's back to get her moving.

They all start walking in the direction of the thrones. As they move, the crowd separates and makes a direct path to the queen. A small orb of soft light suddenly appears over the queen's head, and Trudy sees the face of Danielle incased. She quickly looks around to see if anyone else sees what she is seeing. No one seems to notice the orb except Trudy. Danielle smiles at her, and Trudy remembers their conversation from last night and immediately feels comforted; as soon as that happens, the orb disappears.

The group stands in front of the royal couple with the fairies at their sides. Lilly addresses the queen and king: "Great Mother and Great Father, may I introduce these outer-world visitors to you?" Lilly turns slightly and swings her right hand out, bows her head, and then looks to Trudy. The queen and king broaden their smiles and nod.

"This is Trudy." Lilly looks back over her left shoulder at the queen.

"Welcome, Trudy," both of the royals say in unison.

"Hello." Trudy barely gets the word out.

Lilly then flies to Adele, Richie, Jeff, and Doni, introducing them in the same polite manner, and the queen and king greet each of them with a warm welcome and smile.

The Great Mother then steps forward. "We are grateful that you have chosen to visit us; we have so much to share with you." She sweeps her arms out in a gesture to include everyone in the room; all are staring at her with great respect and love. "All of us want the outer world to know of our work here; however, in the past centuries, the residents of your world have closed their ears and minds to us, and in so doing, they have closed their minds to the inherent nature of the earth. Most have not heard Mother Earth's cries for help in keeping her healthy and strong so that she may in turn protect and take care of all Earth's inhabitants. We invite you to come and learn about us and to enjoy this gathering. Please feel free to talk to as many of our residents as possible. Get to know us and feel comfortable with us, for we have much to show you." She then smiles again at everyone and gracefully sits down on her throne.

The king takes her hand in his and then nods toward the visitors, saying, "It is time to celebrate!" The music then gets louder, joyous voices rise, and the laughter continues.

The tables are decorated with bowls of apples, nuts, and all types of berries. There are bowls of candy and large pitchers of milk, along with many trays of tiny cakes.

Topsy and Doni become friends right away. Topsy grabs the ribbed collar of Doni's shirt and pulls him to the cake table. He then hands

Doni a piece of the chocolate cake. "Here, try this cake. You'll love it! I'll pour you some milk to go with it." Topsy takes Doni to a nearby table and sits him down, putting a wooden cup of milk in front of him. Doni takes a bite of his cake, and with his mouth full, he announces that it is the best cake he has ever had! "I told you! I told you!" Topsy sings out, and then he proceeds to get both of them more of everything.

Jeff and Richie decide to take a tour around the great hall with the help of Jamie. Richie writes down everything he sees, while Jeff tries to draw a few diagrams so that he won't forget where everything is. He is going to try to figure out where this place is in comparison to the outer world. Right at this moment, he figures that they are somewhere under and around Grandma Maya's house, even though he can't see it.

Adele and Trudy sit at a small table with the fairies. They are served nuts, berries, and cakes, along with some wine, which they decline. They do, however, greedily drink the milk that is brought to them; it is the best they have ever had.

"This is a lovely party," Trudy says. "Do you throw a party for everyone who visits here?"

"Well, not everyone," answers Lilly. "Some come here for the wrong reasons."

Adele looks surprised. "Wrong reasons? What kind of wrong reasons?"

Magdalena answers, "Some people sneak in here with the idea of catching one of us. They would like to cage us and show us off for money!" She stomps her foot in midair, causing her wings to move so quickly that they become almost invisible; the movement makes her start to ascend as she speaks.

"That's terrible!" Adele tries to keep eye contact with her. "Do they ever succeed?"

Maggie moves forward and, in a soft voice, says, "Yes, someone has taken my brother." She sighs. "And we don't know who has him or where he is."

"I'm sorry," Trudy and Adele say at the same time.

"Once in a great while, these things happen." Everyone turns toward the sound of this sweet voice. At the head of the table stands the queen. "It is a terrible loss."

Blossom quickly gets a chair. "Please sit down and join us, Mother."

The queen sits down and smiles as the fairies bring her refreshments. She then addresses Trudy and Adele: "Are you enjoying yourselves?"

"Oh yes!" they both gush. Then Trudy adds, "This is such a beautiful place; it's hard to believe it's here. I mean, well, I don't understand how it can be hidden from the rest of the world."

"At one time, it was not hidden. All beings on Earth were together and lived in a harmonious and loving way; of course, that was a very long time ago, before recorded history. All of Earth's inhabitants worked and played together, enjoying their lives. We all helped in keeping the earth beautiful, and she, our Mother Earth, in turn gave us everything we needed; it was a glorious time." The queen takes a sip from her tiny wooden cup and smiles up at the girls.

"Were you alive then? I mean, do you actually remember the time that you are telling us about?" Adele is not quite sure how to ask her question politely.

The queen smiles. "I have lived a very long time, but the times that I refer to are in the collective memory that all of the earth's elementals share. Some of us live an extremely long time in Earth years; however, the times that I speak of are so long ago that no elementals alive today were actually there. We inherit our memories; it is a gift that we all share. We remember both the good and the bad, and as each one of us dies, we leave our memories as an inheritance to all of our people; you can imagine how big that gift grows as the years move on. It is part of the web of life that keeps us all connected."

"Queen Mother," says Trudy, "I feel that I was drawn here. I think Lilly let me see her so I would follow her here with my friends. Is this true?"

Upon hearing this, Lilly flies to Trudy, puts her hand on Trudy's shoulder, and smiles. "It's true. You were invited to come here and bring your friends. We've watched you play around our entryway, and we've seen you many times at Maya's house. We've listened to your conversations and watched your actions, and we believe that you can help us connect with the outer world again in a good and loving way."

The queen then says, "The earth is in need of help, and we cannot do it alone anymore. The problem has become too big for any one group to do the work individually. We need each other. For years now, we have attempted to work with the caring people of Earth, who, in their own ways, take on the struggles of keeping the earth beautiful, but humans get in the way of each other and find it difficult to stay on task. We feel that we need to reach the hearts of people in a more compatible way, so we have decided to do that by reaching out to their children. The human heart has always cared about the children and their future, and that is why we are reaching out to you and your friends—in the hope that more people of Earth will listen and follow your lead."

Trudy is stunned. How can she tell this elemental queen that she can't help? Who is going to listen to her or her friends? Her parents might listen, but who is going to listen to her parents? She feels a knot grow in her stomach, and as she grabs at it, she turns to look at Adele, who is already staring back with a bewildered look. Adele then widens her eyes and shrugs in answer to Trudy's glance.

"You can help. You are very powerful children; you just don't know it yet." The queen is answering their unspoken questions. "You don't know how to access your powers—that's all—and we will teach you that. That is why we invited you here—to teach you all that you will need to know." She smiles at them.

"Hey, what time is it?" Adele interrupts. "Don't we have to go home? Isn't your mom having the neighborhood potluck tonight? Don't we have to help?" She then addresses the queen: "We had a lovely time here. Thank you for everything, but we've gotta go." Adele stands up and pulls on Trudy's collar. "Thanks again for showing us this magical place." Adele bows her head slightly toward the queen.

"There's no need to rush." The queen gestures for Adele to sit back down. "We do not have time here as you know it. Only seconds have passed in the outer world since you have been here. You have plenty of time. I promise you will not be late to your party. Please sit and enjoy your food and drink. It was not my wish to scare you. I wanted you to know that you were asked to come here for a purpose that we know you can fulfill, even if you don't feel capable of that right now. You children of Earth are powerful beings, and you can change the world—and we will teach you how."

The king walks over to the table and puts his strong hands on the shoulders of the queen, and as she feels his hands, she turns to look up at him. A strong feeling of love passes through their gaze, and everyone at the table can feel it; it is commanding and gentle all at the same time. "Are you enjoying our hospitality?" He looks directly at the girls. "We are pleased that you are here, and my hope is that you will come back often to visit us." He smiles at them. He notices the questionable looks on both of their faces and then looks down at his queen. "Dancing Waters, what have you been talking about?"

Dancing Waters looks into the king's large brown eyes. "Gentle Mountain Lion, my king, we have been discussing the purpose of their visit and why it is so important to us. I have just explained to them that they have the power to change the world and that it is our hope they will learn from us and teach others to help."

"I see." His kind eyes are once again looking at the girls. "There are many things that we can teach you—many things that were once known to the outer world but have been cast to the wayside. Why this is so, we do not really understand; nonetheless, your kind has not acted upon this knowledge for many centuries, and it is our desire as the guardians of nature to pass this knowledge on to the human children so that they may now act on it." His face has grown stern, yet it keeps its kindness and love as he speaks.

Both Trudy and Adele feel butterflies in their stomachs; they are excited—and frightened—at being chosen to do something special.

Topsy and Doni have finished eating and are approaching the table where Trudy and Adele sit with the king and queen. Doni notices the looks on his friends' faces.

"What's going on?" he asks as he sits down at the table.

The king turns to answer him. "We are discussing the reason that you've been allowed to come here."

Gentle Mountain Lion puts his hand upon Doni's arm and pats him. This touch makes Doni feel extremely strong throughout his entire body. It is a great feeling! Doni then raises his arms to look like a bodybuilder and flexes his muscles at the girls, causing everyone to giggle a bit. "I'm ready to do anything you want!"

"That is good." The king looks pleased.

Topsy then flies up to the king and flexes his muscles. "Me too!" he squeaks.

Everyone laughs a little harder at Topsy's cute moves, which makes him feel a little shy, and he turns a bit red in the face.

The queen puts her hand out to him. "We know we can always count on you, Topsy."

Her words make Topsy feel so excited and happy that he flies quickly upward and does a backflip.

"Wow!" yells Doni. "That was really cool!"

The queen then stands up and takes the hand of her king. "We will talk again later, after you've had a chance to look around and talk with others here. And remember that you have plenty of time, and we will not allow you to be late getting home." She and the king walk slowly into the crowd of partiers, greeting everyone graciously.

Richie, Jeff, Doni, Adele, and Trudy have a wonderful time meeting all of the different types of personalities at the party. While they walk around the great room, Trudy takes the opportunity to talk to Richie and Jeff. She tells them what the queen and king told them. Richie writes down everything while Trudy talks, and Jeff makes thoughtful faces and comments to hide his mixture of excitement and awe.

The fairies take turns introducing them to all who are there, including the animals. The animals do not speak, but they move in ways that the children understand as answers. It is amazing! Trudy remarks to Adele that she thinks her own dog, Tinkerbelle, always understands her, but for her to feel that all animals here understand her is quite thrilling; she loves animals so very much!

"They are wonderful!" Lilly pats the back of a small unicorn as she speaks; the unicorn touches Lilly sweetly with his muzzle.

Trudy rubs the unicorn's nose lightly and then turns to Maggie, who is standing on the animal's rump. "Could our dogs come here?"

"Of course, if they wanted to. They do come here on occasion; all of the pets in your neighborhood visit us now and then, and they know that you are here now. However, this time of year, since they help us by guarding our entryway, they don't usually visit."

Adele looks puzzled. "Why do they need to guard the tree?"

"During this time of year, our entryway is more vulnerable to unseemly visitors. It is easier to find the passageway, and although we welcome most visitors, there are some who would cause us trouble. Your pets have agreed to guard our entry, and in this process, it makes for a safer visit for you. They love you all very much."

Trudy looks surprised. "You know our pets, and they know that we are here?"

"Yes. Yes," Maggie sings out. "They are wonderful and full of fun. We all know them and love it when they visit us!"

"Do you know Grandma Maya and Henry too?" asks Trudy.

"Yes. Maya has never been here, but she has caught glimpses of us. She knows we are here. We talk to her while she is in her garden. She hears us as thoughts that are not her own. We help her garden grow, and she allows us to move about her land without fear. We love her willingness to keep her land open to us and to the plants and animals that live there. We are lucky to have her so close to our entryway. Others around the world have not been so lucky. Their entryways have been crushed or ruined in a way that they cannot be used anymore. The animals in these areas need us to help them survive, but we can't get to them. This is another reason we need your help."

"Well, I want to help, but I don't know what to do."

"Not to worry," says Maggie. She takes the girls' hands, and together they join the rest of the party.

Jamie follows Jeff and Richie as they wander off from the main hall. They are curious to see what else is in this hollow tree. They discover a hallway behind the thrones and want to see where it goes.

"Do you think we should go back here?" Richie asks as they approach their destination.

"Why not?" Jeff keeps walking as he talks. "They said we could go anywhere, and there are no guards or anything. We aren't hurting anything. You worry too much." Jeff slows a bit and proceeds cautiously.

"They told us to enjoy the party, which was not an invitation to sneak around back here." Richie does not want to offend his hosts.

Jeff stops and looks at Richie. "Well, if you don't want to come, then go back to the party. I'm just looking around. I'll see you later." Jeff walks on, and Richie quickly follows.

"Oh, wow! Look at this."

Richie looks over to where Jeff is standing, and he watches as Jeff bends down in front of a tiny door—at least it appears to be a door.

Jeff gets down on his hands and knees. "Listen. Can you hear that?" He puts his ear to the door without waiting for an answer. "It's a funny kind of sound," he whispers.

Just as Jeff puts his ear to the door, it swings open, surprising him. A tiny man comes through the doorway; he is about as tall as a large man's thumb. He wears something that looks like what a caveman would wear, only it is made of pounded and softened bark. His skin is a ruddy dark brown, his feet are covered with strange ankle-high boots, and his curly black hair is shoulder length and messy. He stands with his fists tight to his hips and stares up at Jeff with a bemused look on his face. "What's your business here?" His voice is deeper than expected for such a small man.

Jeff falls backward onto his bottom. He is completely bewildered by the sight of this miniature man, and so is Richie. Both boys have their eyes riveted on the figure before them, and their mouths are wide open, but neither can say anything. As they watch the man, he starts to grow before them, growing to the size of a small child.

"I said what's your business here?"

Then they hear the voice of Jamie whisper, "Say something nice quickly, or he'll go back!"

"Aha ... okay." But before Richie can answer, he hears Jeff speak.

"Who are you? Why aren't you at the party?"

The man is clearly annoyed at this response. "What's your business, boy?" Jeff points up to Richie. "We're just looking around this place like the queen told us to." Jeff stands up, brushing off the back of his pants and smiling down at the fierce little man.

"The queen sent you here?" he questions. "Why would she send you to me, boy? You can't get in here!" He points to the tiny door. "Are you telling me a falsehood?"

Jamie flies up to the man. "These are my friends, Tom." He points to the boys. "This is Jeff, and this is Richie. I'm Richie's muse," he explains. "They were just looking around and found your door; they are interested in all of us, and they just wanted to meet you." Jamie's smile grows larger as he speaks.

"They knew that I was here? They came to meet me? Highly unlikely, Jamie, but I'll be nice." Tom steps out farther into the hallway, brushing Jamie aside. Jeff bends down and shakes Tom's hand and is surprised at the strength of Tom's hold.

Richie slowly walks over and does the same, putting on his best smile. "Nice to meet you, sir." This gesture seems to please Tom, so Richie continues, "We are visiting here today, and we thought we'd have a look around; we did not mean to disturb you."

Tom feels that Richie is polite, and the boy's attempt at being gracious softens him. In spite of the way that Tom appears, he is, at heart, a good elf. He takes his work seriously and does not like to be disturbed. He feels that work is as important as play, and he puts his all into everything he does.

Jeff notices an earthy smell coming from Tom. It seems to be a plant smell. "What do you do in there, Tom? I heard a noise that sounded like a light pounding."

Tom cocks his head to the side, looks up into Jeff's eyes, and then slowly looks toward Richie and Jamie. Jamie is sitting on Richie's shoulder. "I make paper. Well, I mean that my family—my tribe—makes paper. We use an abundant plant from the outer world that grows in Africa. We are trying to communicate the making of this paper to your people, but they are not, as yet, ready. We can save many trees by making paper in this way. The trees are the earth's lungs, you know. They must be saved. They are here to give us beauty and shelter and comfort. Look at how beautiful this small door is. It is a work of art made out of the strong wood of an oak. It gives much pleasure to all who use it. I wasn't expecting to tell you this on your first visit here. There are other ideas that you need to learn about first."

This last comment catches the boys off guard; they think this is a once-in-a-lifetime visit, and this elf is talking to them as if they are going to go to school here or, at the very least, visit more than once.

"What are you talking about?" Jeff looks concerned. "We're just supposed to look around and talk to some of you. This wasn't a planned visit, you know. No one knew that we were coming. We didn't even know until it happened." Then Jeff remembers what Trudy told him, and although he'd listened to all that she said, he hadn't gotten the picture until right now. "You make it sound as if you all knew that we would be here today. There's no real way that you could have known this." He turns to look at his friend. "Right, Richie?"

Richie stops writing in his notebook and looks up at Jeff. He doesn't know what to say, so he shrugs and lifts one eyebrow to express his semisurprise at the notion that they are here to learn something.

Then Tom breaks in. "Well, nonetheless, you will be coming back to learn from us. It's in the geodes." Tom starts to shrink back down to his original size, and when he reaches it, he steps back into the doorway. He sticks his head out to nod good-bye and pulls the door closed.

When the boys hear the lock click, they turn to look at each other.

Then Jeff speaks to Jamie. "What did he mean by saying it was in the geodes?"

Jamie tries to answer quickly. "We keep information in our geodes like you can keep information in your computers."

Both Richie and Jeff look at Jamie, surprised.

Then Jeff speaks. "Are you saying that there is information in rocks that you guys use to tell the future?"

"Yes. But it's not all futuristic; some of the information is what has happened in the past as well. Come on. Let's go. There's more to see." Jamie tugs on Richie's collar.

"No. No. No!" Jeff shakes his head and looks at Jamie. "What's going on? Why does everyone assume that we are returning to this place to learn something? We haven't made any decisions. We haven't even finished this visit! And what's with the geodes?"

Jamie doesn't want to get into all this by himself. He feels that others can answer these questions a lot better than he can, but now he has no choice. "Well, um, it's kind of like your library system, I guess."

"What is?" insists Jeff. In his anger, he has lost track of his questions.

"The geodes—they hold pertinent information like computer storage. It's in the crystals. We can hold them in our hands and put them to our foreheads and learn from them telepathically."

Jeff just stares at Jamie and then back at Richie. "All this is crazy! All I want to know right now is how everyone seems to know us and why everyone thinks that we're coming back. We can discuss the geodes later." He pauses and then adds, "I guess." Jeff shakes his head in irritation.

Richie takes Jamie off of his shoulder and holds him in front of his face by holding on to Jamie's wings. "He acted as if we had already agreed to return, Jamie. Why? We haven't agreed to anything that I know of. Is there some kind of plan to keep us here?" He drops Jamie into his other hand.

"Plan?" A huge grin appears on Jamie's face as he speaks. "I don't know of any plan, Richie." Jamie starts to lift off of Richie's hand. "We knew that you were coming, but ..." Jamie darts off, not finishing his thought.

"Come back!" Richie orders, but it does no good; Jamie is out of sight.

"Come on, Jeff." Richie starts walking back out of the hallway. "Let's find the girls and Doni; we gotta talk."

8

Richie and Jeff round up their friends and have them sit together at a table near the back of the thrones in the main hall.

Jeff starts. "Does anyone know what's really going on here? Did you understand that they believe that we are returning? Did you know that they"—Jeff points out to the crowd of partiers—"think this trip was planned? Which, by the way, would be impossible since we didn't even know that we would be coming here and didn't know that we would be running in to you when we were fishing. So there were no plans that I know of!" Jeff is pacing back and forth as he speaks; his arms are waving about, and his head is shaking. Everyone can see that he is upset by all of this.

"Calm down, Jeff." Trudy jumps up and grabs on to one of his arms. "We're all okay, so calm down! No one is hurting us." Then she says in a soft whisper, "Sit down and relax."

Jeff sits down between Trudy and Adele. He puts his head in his hands and sighs. "Just tell me what's going on."

"Please don't be upset." The sweet, soft voice of Lilly is suddenly there. Everyone looks up to where they hear the voice and are a bit surprised to see not only Lilly but also all of the other fairies and Jamie staring back at them. "We truly are your friends. We won't harm any of you. We promise." Lilly is sincere, and so are all of the others as they nod in agreement. "Please calm down, and I'll try to explain what is going on."

Trudy takes the hands of Adele and Jeff, who take the hands of the others, as a sign of unity, support, and love for each other. Doni is the only one not upset by what is happening. He is completely relaxed and loves being in this magical place. His friend Topsy is standing behind him with his hand on Doni's shoulder.

Lilly begins, "We've watched all of you for a long while, and we've seen how good all of you are toward our small forest. We've seen how you treat the animals and each other. We've seen how the birds are attracted to Jeff and how they come and sit with him when no one is around to see." She smiles toward Jeff. The others are surprised by this statement and all turn to look at Jeff too. He has an astonished look on his face; he thought that no one had ever seen him sit with the birds, except Richie.

Lilly continues, "We have watched and listened to all of you, and we know that with a little encouragement and some training, you can work with us to help save Mother Earth."

Jeff looks up at Lilly. "But how did you know for sure that we would come here? We didn't know until it happened, yet you keep saying that you knew we would be here. I just don't understand."

"It's very hard to explain what knowing is, but we have a sense that tells us what will happen and when. You humans have this knowing also; you call it intuition. Our knowing is stronger than your intuition because we use it all of the time. Your intuition has lost its power because humans don't really trust to use it and have been thought to ignore it. You are brought up believing that others know what is best for you, so you disregard your inner feelings about things. The truth is that what you believe to be true for you is true for you."

"I'm confused," says Adele. "Are you saying that what we've been taught is all wrong?"

"Oh no." Lilly shakes her head. "Some of the ideas and theories that humans have are wrong. Every person is different; therefore, no one idea or theory can fit every person. However, that is what humans believe to be true." Lilly is searching for the right words. "Here is an example: humans feel that certain emotions should be changed if the emotion is deemed as inappropriate to the majority of humans, and that is because humans have designated feelings for certain events, and when these natural feelings are replaced with taught feelings, you will eventually lose your natural feelings, your intuition." Lilly knows she isn't explaining this correctly.

"I still don't understand," says Adele, and the others nod in agreement.

Maggie takes Lilly's hand. "Let me try." Lilly agrees.

"Adele, remember when your grandfather died?"

"Yes." Adele is a bit put off by this question.

"Do you recall the moment that you thought you saw him during the funeral service?"

Adele had pushed that memory away and is caught off guard when Maggie brings it up, so she is hesitant in her answer. "Yes, I was sitting next to my mother, and I saw Poppy standing right in front of me. He was putting his finger in front of his mouth and smiling at me. I knew that he was telling me not to speak and that he came to let me know that he loved me and that everything would be all right."

"That's right!" Maggie is excited that Adele remembers the incident. "What happened next?"

"I was giggling at the face my poppy was making at me and feeling happy that he was with me, when my mother leaned into me and angrily whispered for me to be quiet. She said that I was acting inappropriately. She said that I should be sad. My poppy then disappeared. Later, when I tried to tell my mother what had happened in church, she got mad at me and told me it was just my imagination, which made me feel sad for a very long time." She wipes a tear from her cheek. "And I never saw my grandfather, my poppy, again."

"This is an example of how humans are trained to get rid of their intuition, their knowing. Adele, you knew when you saw your grandfather that he was okay, and that made you feel happy because you knew that he wasn't truly gone—he was with you. However, when you were told to stop having that feeling, you felt that you were doing something wrong. You felt wrong because you were disappointing your mother and confused by having the good feeling of seeing your grandfather and knowing that he was fine. He was just in another dimension that is not visible to all humans— that's all. So you did what you were told to do, and in doing so, you started the process of shutting down your intuition, your knowing abilities. You couldn't see your grandfather anymore. The hardest part of this to grasp is that your mother was just doing what she thought was the right thing to do. It was what she was taught to do. She has been taught to not listen to her gut feelings, and she is trying to teach you to do the same."

Adele jumps up from her seat, knocking it over, and bursting into tears, she yells out, "She loves me!"

The fairies fly to her side to comfort her.

"Of course she loves you!" Orange Blossom pats Adele's free hand; the other hand is still holding on to Trudy.

"Oh, I'm so sorry. I'm not saying any of this to hurt you. I know that your mother has a huge heart full of love for you. She was trained, as were so many others, by fear disguised as love. She did what she did because she loves you and wants what is best for you. She wants you to fit in and be accepted by other humans. This has gone on for many centuries; the blocking of your natural instincts started many generations ago. It is not your fault or the fault of your loved ones. It's just what has happened. Fear is the culprit, certainly not love!" Maggie goes to Adele and hugs her.

Trudy is equally confused. "Why are people so fearful? What caused this fear in the first place?"

"I don't know the first cause of fear—probably the same thing that caused the first lie. Disappointment? Not wanting to disappoint someone you love may cause people to fear their loved ones' disapproval, I guess. No one likes to be judged like that. We are all born different. No one sees the world the same way in all things. What one person sees as a good thing, another person may see as a bad thing, and there would still be others who would not be concerned about this thing at all. This is a world of extreme opposites, you know, with many degrees in between."

"No, I don't know!" Adele picks up her chair and sits down with a thud, crossing her arms in an angry way.

Maggie speaks in her most compassionate voice. "What is the opposite of cold?"

"Hot!" yells out Doni. He loves to play word games.

Maggie smiles at Doni. "That's correct, Doni. However, there are many degrees of temperature in between hot and cold. Are there not?"

Everyone nods, except Adele, whose eyes stay glued to Maggie.

Maggie continues, "What is the opposite of dark?"

"Light!" This time, everyone answers except Adele.

"Correct, but there are also many different types of light in between, right?"

Again, they all nod.

Then, looking straight back at Adele, Maggie asks, "What, then, would be the opposite of love?"

"Hate," Adele answers.

"And what causes hate?"

Richie answers in a low voice, "I think it is fear, and there are many degrees of fear and love."

"Why, yes!" says Maggie, a bit surprised. "You came up with this answer quickly."

"Yeah." Jeff has an unconfirmed look.

"How did you come up with that so fast?"

"I hate ants, and I used to love them. Well, I mean, I used to love my ant farm," Richie explains. "I loved to watch the little ants work. I couldn't wait to get home from school to see the new paths that they had built while I was away. It was fun. Then, one night, I got up to use the bathroom, and I knocked the farm over and broke it by mistake. The ants got everywhere, even in my bed. It was gross! They got into my desk, and they were all over my bedroom. It totally creeped me out! I cleaned my bedroom from top to bottom because I was afraid of them. I didn't want them in my stuff or on my bed. I didn't want them on me at night when I was sleeping. I began to hate them, and every time I saw one, I would kill it. My feelings went from love to fear to hate. They were still the same ants, but now I hated them! I went from letting them crawl on my hand at times to stepping on them even if they were outside."

Richie's friends are all staring at him—not because of the story but because they don't remember Richie ever saying so much at one time.

Trudy breaks the short silence. "You had ants in your bedroom? Yuck!" She makes an awful face at him.

"I remember when that happened!" Doni laughs. "We had ants all over the house! Mom was really mad! We all hate ants! My mom has ant traps everywhere."

Everyone giggles a bit, but Orange Blossom doesn't want Richie to feel that his story is just for laughs, so she addresses him in an earnest way. "Your story is a good one, Richie. It explains, in a very simple way, how love, hate, and fear are conjured up and how hate can spread from one person to another. You shared your room with the ants for a while, and everything was fine—until their home was disturbed. They, of course, were just doing what ants do, but you and your family had some obvious differences with them in how they should live. You live your life in a certain manner, so the ants could not coexist with you in your bedroom or in your house without the ant farm to keep them in. The problem was not with the ants or with you. The problem was that the ants could not live in your bedroom without being contained in the ant farm. They did not have a choice in what happened to them, so they did what comes naturally to ants. Therefore, your conclusion should have been that ants and people live differently, not that every ant you see should be killed. But the fear you had of the ants turned into hate, and now you are teaching others to fear and hate ants because of your actions. These actions cause others to be influenced by your experience. If others like you, or love you, they tend to believe what they are experiencing with you—they trust you. People share stories with those they love, and some of these stories are told to protect each other out of love for one another. No matter how misguided some of these conclusions may be, people see the intent as good. Even though these others have never had your experience, they would kill ants because they feel your good intent for them in telling them that the ants are bad. They would then teach others to kill ants, even though they had never had a bad experience with them. Then others would join in—those who had never heard your story but were told that ants were bad and should be killed. This is not a judgment on whether ants are good or bad, but an explanation of how it is possible for people to believe something because they are taught it and not because they have experienced it for themselves."

Maggie sits on the table in front of Adele. "So if someone saw a spirit that had died and was frightened by it, they would be telling a story of fear to those they loved, and if enough people concluded that it was a bad thing to see the spirits of those that have died, then those encounters would be seen as bad. Since most people do not want to be seen as bad, they would start to ostracize those that reported seeing spirits, teaching others that people who saw spirits were bad. Then this would be the start of blocking out the knowing that they had been born with. This has gone on for many, many generations. In most cases, people don't even know why they are taught to do the things that they do. They just do them because the people they love do them. Your mother was only doing what she did because of her love for you and her desire to teach you what she believes to be true and good. She did not want people to see you giggling in church during your grandfather's funeral, because she deemed it as not being respectful to the moment, and she refused to believe that you saw your poppy, because he was dead, which to her meant that he was truly gone. She was honoring her beliefs and passing them on to you, like many generations before."

"Everyone is born with the gift of knowing," Blossom adds, "but many humans are taught that it is a curse and not a gift, and then they lose it. Children are told that they are only seeing an imaginary friend when they tell their parents of their sight, and that surely diminishes the experience of a child's play."

This last statement by Blossom strikes Trudy, and she feels that she needs to talk about her encounters with her angel, so she just blurts it out: "I see my guardian angel." Everyone turns to look at her. "She comes to me at night sometimes, and I saw her here today."

"You saw her today?" asks Adele.

"Yes. I saw her appear over the queen and king earlier." As Trudy is answering, she sees the orb of pearlescent light, and she feels the warmth of love throughout her body that always occupies her when she sees her angel. She points to the orb. "Look! There she is. Do you see her?"

Everyone looks to where Trudy is pointing, and they all see the orb getting larger and larger. The shimmering pink-and-white light sends off a loving feeling to all of them. They can see a face emerge in the center; it is beautiful! The angelic face is smiling at them and generating a feeling of protection around all of them. The angel does not speak, but she lets them know that they are all being protected by their own guardian angels. She also lets them know that Trudy's gift of sight is well developed and should be respected. All stand up in silence; even the fairies are quiet. The angel then showers them with love, which looks like white, blue, and pink fireworks shooting from her orb, but there is no sound. When the sparks of light touch their skin, it is exciting and warm. The fairies' wings start to move quickly, and the fairies themselves start to spin, which makes a lovely, musical sound that breaks the silence. The orb starts to recede and slowly disappears into a tiny dot that then zips away like a shooting star.

The great hall is quiet for a moment, and then the party starts up again.

"Wow!" Doni gushes. "Do you get to see her all of the time?"

"No." Trudy sits back down, and so do the rest of the party as they look to her for a more complete answer. "But I think that she is around me all of the time. It's easier for me to see her at night, though."

"Do you talk to her?" Richie is pulling his pad and pencil out to record the answer.

"Not really talk—she already knows what I am thinking. I think. When she answers me, she doesn't talk by using her mouth; she thinks things to me, and it sounds like my own voice talking, but I know it's her. Sometimes I talk out loud to her, and she will always answer me, even if I don't see her."

"She's very beautiful!" Adele gives Trudy a delighted look and takes her hand again. "She made me feel safe and relaxed."

Topsy's small voice breaks in. "You all have an angel. Every earthling has a guardian. Isn't it wonderful?"

"Everybody?" Jeff is dubious. "Even bad people?"

"Well," Magdalena breaks in, "they have them, but they do not acknowledge them. If people do not listen to their angels, then the angels cannot help them, and they will eventually push their angels away. This is called a loss of conscience. Angels cannot interfere with one's life unless they are asked to. They cannot help you if you do not ask them to. There are also times when angels are asked to help, but their help is ignored because it is not what the person wants to hear or because the information comes as intuition and they do not believe it. So the advice, or help, is disregarded as their own thoughts and not the help that they have asked for."

"Why wouldn't they believe it, if it is the answer to their problem?" asks Jeff.

"The same reason that you do not always believe, Jeff—because the information may come in your thoughts with your own voice, in a dream that you feel strongly about, or even through another human. The answers in life do not come easily. If they did, we would never learn anything. You must learn to trust. Do you understand?"

"I guess so—a little maybe."

"I get it!" announces Doni. "It's like when we do something a million times that we knew in our brain that we shouldn't be doing, and we don't get caught or in trouble or even hurt. But then, one day, we do it, and we get hurt really bad or get into big trouble or both because we weren't listening to ourselves, our angels. We were just listening to our ..." Doni stops; he doesn't know what to say next. "What is it that we listen to when bad things happen?"

"It's your human voice—the voice that wants to learn and have fun. It's not a bad voice, Doni; it's your own voice. Your own voice may override your intuition at any time because we all have free will."

Richie looks up from his notepad. "The hard part is knowing which voice and which choice are yours, right?"

"Yes. Yes!" agrees Magdalena. "But you can tell if you truly listen. You will know."

"It's a feeling in your stomach, a kind of knot," explains Lilly, "when something is wrong or just not quite right. You've all had that feeling. Haven't you?"

They all nod.

"The feeling doesn't explain things in detail. It won't tell you exactly what you should do—that decision is up to you—but if you continuously override these feelings, you will eventually stop feeling them, and if you ever what them to come back, you will have to work very hard at it. New parents get this feeling when they have a child, and if they truly work at it, this knowing—intuition—can be very helpful to them. The bonds of love are very strong, so if you put love into all that you do, this knowing will come to you."

Richie looks up from his writing. "Lilly, if something is fun to do but you've been taught not to do it, is it bad? I mean, if you're not hurting anyone or anything, just having fun, and you don't get a bad feeling about it, is your intuition involved?"

"Now you're getting away from our discussion; however, I will answer this in the context of feelings only. I will make it as simple as I can. Let's say that you've been taught to ride your bike wearing a helmet, and you choose to ride your bike without your helmet. Now, there may be many reasons that you choose to do this, and all of them seem valid in your opinion, but to ride your bike without your helmet will endanger your safety. With a helmet, you are safer than without a helmet—that's it. It is not good or bad; it safe or not safe. So you choose to not wear your helmet, but every time you use your bike, you think about your helmet and ignore your feelings until, eventually, you hardly notice them at all. The feeling was telling you that you should protect yourself, but it is not the same as the feelings of good and bad. You may feel bad that you are not following what you were taught; however, the wind in your hair as you ride your bike may feel very good, so it is fun to ride your bike this way. These are not the true feelings of intuition. Intuition is not a fear of getting into trouble or a dread of punishment if caught doing something wrong. It is not a reward for doing good either; there are no attached feelings to intuition except the gut feeling that you must take action. It is the knowing that you are doing what is the right thing for you—that is what motivates your thoughts and actions, not fear, rejection, anger, or reward. You can have intuition about other people, places, and things, but you must believe in yourself first. For intuition to grow, it must be honored."

"Then you're saying that the reason Trudy can see her guardian angel is because she honors the fact that she can do it?"

"Yes. She believes. She was not taught that she can't. Her parents brushed it off as childhood imagination, but they never made it good or bad for Trudy. She was never told that is wasn't true, so Trudy kept honoring what she felt and saw, causing her intuition to grow and become very strong, and that is why she can see her angel." Lilly looks approvingly at Trudy, causing her to blush a bit.

Will and Phil appear in the middle of the large, round table, and both are eager to talk. Phil starts. "It is a mighty power that we all have, but some choose to toss it away and never use it!"

Then Will breaks in, putting his hand on his brother's shoulder. He adds, "We want each of you to use your powers to help the earth and all of her inhabitants. This is why you are here. We will instruct you in the ways of nature to increase your powers of perception and activate your inner strength so that you can go back and teach your people; then we can all work together to save our beautiful Mother Earth."

A smaller yet stronger voice takes over, but they cannot see the body. "We've been watching you all very carefully for a long time, and we know you will help us out. We also knew how to get your attention and how to get you here." It is Ansel, the elf they saw earlier riding on Toby the turtle with his family. He jumps up onto the table, putting his fists on his hips. He looks straight into Trudy's eyes and says, "You are the leader. You know that you have power. You just don't speak of it to the others. You have not yet been taught to block your power out, as they have. Maya has helped you as much as she can. It is now our job to help you and your friends to strengthen your powers that be. You must listen to us, Trudy. You and your friends and those you will soon teach are the hope of the earth."

9

Everyone sits quietly at the table; the fairies and Ansel have left them so that they can have time to take everything they have seen and heard into consideration. Richie is writing in his notebook, but the rest of them are looking to Trudy and waiting for her to speak. Trudy is staring blankly ahead; she looks a bit dazed, but she is thinking about the entire day.

Doni breaks the silence. "What are your secret powers? Does your angel give you power?"

"I don't really know," Trudy replies honestly. "I guess the fact that I can see my angel gives me some power, but I don't really know what kind of power."

Adele then speaks. "Do you have that intuition that they were talking about?"

"I guess. I mean, I do get that feeling in my stomach sometimes, but I thought that I was getting it from Tinkerbelle, my dog." She sees the puzzled look on everyone's face, so she adds, "Well, when I'm planning to do something that maybe I shouldn't, I get that knotted feeling in my stomach, and when that happens, Tinker is usually looking at me like she knows what I'm thinking, so I always thought that it was my dog talking to me like my angel talks to me—brain to brain, not using words." She turns to Adele for acknowledgment.

Adele does know what she is talking about, and she nods slowly. She feels that her little dachshund, Tiny, is always trying to communicate with her too, but she doesn't want to say so out loud.

Jeff looks at the two of them and feels frustrated. "How are we going to be the hope of the earth with that?" He is starting to get angry. "None of this makes any sense. I get that feeling once in a while also, but I don't get how this is going to help anyone else or save the planet."

Richie looks up from his writing. "They said that they would teach us. I think that we should do it. What have we got to lose? Everyone has been nice to us, and they said that we could leave at any time, so I say we should believe them and try to learn what they have to teach us."

"Yeah! Let's stay!" Doni cheers his brother on.

"I don't have any bad feelings about this at all." Trudy stands up and puts her hands on her stomach. "I actually feel very good about all of this. I'll stay!"

"Me too," agrees Adele.

Jeff looks at his friends and shakes his head. He feels that it is his duty to question everything, but he does feel good about being here. The idea that he is being fooled by little beings is kind of silly. Everyone seems to be truthful and kind, so what is there to worry about? "Okay, let's do it!"

The five friends take each other's hands and raise them into the air with a cheer of happiness in their decision to stay and work with the fairies.

"But," Adele says, "we have to be home in time for the party tonight!"

They all laugh as they walk toward the middle of the great hall, holding hands. When they reach the center of the room, they stop; the room has quieted down, and most of the partiers are looking in their direction. Trudy and her friends turn and look in the direction of the thrones and let go of each other's hands. Trudy then steps forward and addresses the king and queen.

Trudy bows her head slightly as she speaks, having seen someone on TV address royalty in this manner. "Queen Dancing Waters and King

Gentle Mountain Lion, my friends and I have decided to stay and learn what you have to teach us. We want to help in any way that we can."

The queen smiles her approval. The king stands to talk. "We are grateful that you have made this decision, and we will get started soon; however, today is a day of rejoicing, so we ask that you stay for a while and celebrate with us. Tomorrow we will start our work together." He then takes the hand of Dancing Waters as she stands up next to him; he raises their arms as the crowd hushes, and he says in a strong voice, "Great Spirit, we thank you for giving us the opportunity to work with our friends of Earth. May we work together as one heart in our endeavors to open the minds of the human race to remind them of their ultimate mission here on this planet." After he completes his prayer, he looks directly into the eyes of Trudy and says, "Thank you."

Trudy is taken aback by the feelings of joy emanating from inside her. She feels like flying. She gives a huge smile back to the royal pair and then turns to her friends to hug them. They all hug each other with the fairies, and the others join in. It is a moment of intense feeling.

Light sprinkles of golden dust are everywhere; the fairies release this dust in moments of great happiness. It comes from their hearts and is released through every pore in their bodies. It is true love.

"Look! Look! Trudy, look!" Adele yells out. "Our feet are off the ground!"

Trudy and the others look down at their feet, and sure enough, they are all a few inches off the ground. They slowly start to swirl, just as they have seen the fairies do. What a glorious feeling! The music starts playing louder, and they all start to dance in midair; even the queen and king are dancing. Trudy can't remember any other time when she has felt this wonderful. She feels as light as a butterfly and as strong as a bear all at the same time, and she feels true love for every living creature of Earth.

Ansel and Darla are dancing with joy next to Trudy and her friends, when they notice Tom standing all by himself in front of the thrones.

Darla whispers to her partner, "What's wrong with Tom? He seems unhappy."

"You know how he is, Darla; he's been through this so many times before."

"Yes, well, haven't we all?"

"I'll go talk to him." Ansel leaves Darla to dance with their son and walks over to Tom.

"Hey, friend, why so glum?" Ansel puts his hand on Tom's shoulder. "You should be enjoying all of this. You've worked so hard to change things. This should be a joyful day for you."

"I guess it should." Tom tries to give Ansel a smile. "I just would hate to see all of my friends let down again." Tom shakes his head sadly. "Do you remember the last time we thought this way? Do you remember how hard we all worked with the others? Do you remember all of the broken promises? I do. I still carry all of this sadness in my heart, Ansel; it hurts, and I can't seem to let it go. It hurts so much."

Ansel can feel Tom's sadness; however, he still carries hope in his heart for all of humankind. He pats Tom's shoulder. "Come, and let's go for a walk outside. The fresh air will do us both good, and we can talk." They walk together down the back corridor and out to the royal gardens. The gardens are rich in plant life and filled with the aroma of wildflowers. The two friends quietly stroll down the stone path that curves in and around the foliage until they reach the latched wooden archway. The panoramic view on the other side of this archway is always breathtaking, no matter how many times it is seen. Ansel thinks that this view will lighten Tom's overburdened heart.

As the companions walk out onto the bluff, their eyes behold a glorious sight. Laid out before them are green rolling hills dotted with lakes, streams, and all types of animals, birds, and vegetation. Far off in the distance rises a majestic mountain range. "Look how beautiful this is, Tom. Wouldn't it be wonderful if the outer world could be this way again? What a gift it would be if we could help them see that things can change."

Tom appreciates his friend's words and gives a small grin. "If this is hard for me, Ansel, and I live here, how much harder is it going to be for the humans? And these humans are young! There are humans that have been trying for many years and have failed, and we have failed to get their attention. I think that the human race just cannot see the dangers ahead for them; they do not see that their concerns for mankind must always include our Mother Earth." Tom sits down on the soft grass and wraps his arms around his bony legs.

Ansel sits down next to Tom. "That is why I think that these young ones will be helpful. The humans will see through the eyes of their future, their offspring, and respond. Love will make it happen!"

Ansel and Tom look into each other's eyes; Ansel nods, and Tom reluctantly nods back. Both elves look out upon the great expanse that lies before them and relax.

"Look," says Ansel, pointing toward the mountains. "You don't see many of them anymore; maybe this is an omen of good luck." There in the distance is a red dragon floating high in the sky. It is so far off that it almost looks black, and although it looks small, it is the largest of its kind. *They are extinct in the outer world and are rarely seen here anymore either,* Ansel thinks. "It is a blessing," he says out loud.

10

It seems as if they have been dancing for hours on end, when Lilly taps Trudy on the shoulder. "It's time for you to return," she says. "We will have a long day tomorrow, and your parents will be expecting you soon."

"Oh! What's the time?" Adele practically shouts out. She instantly becomes worried about being late.

Magdalena flies up to her. "Remember that we do not have time as you know it here. You won't be late; as a matter of fact, you'll be home early!"

The crowd has stopped dancing, and the music is softly playing in the background. Everyone starts to say his or her good-byes, some with words and others with waves. Jamie, Lilly, Maggie, Blossom, Magdalena, Topsy, Will, and Phil are all there, ready to lead them to the exit. As the group approaches the large doors, Trudy can see that the king and queen are waiting for them. Trudy walks directly to them, smiling and feeling as though she can accomplish any task that they may ask of her and her friends.

"Thank you," Trudy says, bowing her head. The others do the same.

"It is us that thank you for your commitment to help us; it is a most wonderful gift that you give Mother Earth," says the queen.

"It is very brave, and it is a valuable service to all," the king says as he shakes their hands in gratefulness. They all feel their chests swell at this notion of being brave.

"Go in peace and love." Gentle Mountain Lion's voice is strong and loving.

They all wave good-bye as they walk through the giant doors toward the stone path that will take them back home.

Everyone is quiet on the trek back. All of them are thinking about the day's events and what will follow. Occasionally, they glance at one another thoughtfully and smile or sigh. The air smells of flowers—fresh and clean. The music stays with them as they walk, and the fairies are happily flying around them, chatting and showing them the way.

Trudy can't shake the feeling that they are being watched; it isn't a bad feeling, just unsettling. She whispers to Adele, "The fox is around us—I can feel it."

"I can feel it too. Should we say something?"

"No, let's see what happens tomorrow, if it's still around."

"Okay."

When they reach the oak passageway, everyone starts to say good-bye. "If it is possible for you to come early tomorrow, it would be good," says Lilly. "There is much we need to teach you."

"And a lot of stuff we want to show you," adds Topsy.

"Well, I don't know what time we'll be back," Trudy says thoughtfully.

"We'll know when you've arrived, and we'll be here to meet you." Maggie kisses Jeff on the forehead. "And we would like all of you to return, if possible." She smiles and looks at Adele.

Adele looks up into Blossom's beautiful little face and just smiles. Adele isn't sure what she wants to do yet.

"Be true to your feelings, Adele; don't let fear get in the way. You can be a great help to all of mankind if your heart is truly in what you are doing, but if you do not want to come back, you shouldn't, because your reluctance and fear will hinder our progress." Then Blossom addresses all of them: "Whatever you choose to do, make sure that it is your choice. If you choose with love, it will be the right choice."

The fairies kiss them all on their foreheads or on the tips of their noses.

"Enter toward the right side," Lilly instructs, and she points toward the entry.

Jeff goes first this time; he walks into the entry, and as he sets his foot down in the twinkling shaft of light, his body takes off, and he starts laughing at the quickness of it. The others follow, and all of them laugh as they take off flying. The feeling is exhilarating. Each one plummets through the passageway. They can each see one another as they travel through the tunnel, and when they make eye contact, they grin at the sight of each other tumbling through the air.

When Jeff reaches the end of the tunnel, he is tossed out onto the mossy ground near the entrance. He then quickly gets up and moves to make way for the others. Everyone lands with a laugh; they are excited to be back. Trudy's and Adele's dogs are there to greet them as they arrive; both of them are barking and jumping up and down with the joy of their friends' return.

Jeff looks skyward and notices that the sun is high in the sky. "Hey, it's only around lunchtime." His voice is veiled in surprise. "We have the whole afternoon to hang out before we need to go home!"

"Let's go to Grandma Maya's house and tell her what's happened." Trudy waves the others on toward the creek as she runs with Tinkerbelle barking at her side.

11

Maya is relaxing on her front porch with a glass of iced tea when she hears the troop of visitors that she has been waiting for coming toward her. Henry jumps up onto the railing to watch as they approach and to ready himself for the dogs he so loves to tease. He arches his back and hisses to get their attention. The dogs race toward him barking, and the game of chase commences.

Jeff and Adele reach the steps to the porch at the same time, breathless and laughing.

"It's wonderful to see all of you! Please come and sit." Maya swings her arm around like a game-show host to show the happy visitors where to sit. Before sitting, they take turns saying hello and giving Maya warm hugs. The two older boys try to be gentle when they hug her so that they won't hurt the old woman. They sit down on the braided rug near the rockers with Trudy. Doni and Adele sit in the chairs next to Maya. On the wicker table is a tray with a pitcher of lemonade and five stacked glasses. "Would you like some lemonade?" Maya is already pouring the first glass.

Doni says yes right away, and the others nod in unison.

Trudy points to the stacked glasses. "How did you know we were coming?"

"When I was fixing my iced tea, I got a feeling and then a picture in my mind that you were going to visit me, so I made some lemonade. It just happens to me sometimes. I believe it is called a premonition." Maya smiles and continues to serve the ice-cold drinks. When she finishes, she asks if they are hungry, and after getting an affirmative nod from the group, she turns and reaches for a dish of apple-butter sandwiches that seem to appear on the same tray.

"That was like magic!" Doni's eyes are open wide as he stares at Maya. "How'd you do that? Where did that dish come from?"

"Right here." Maya smiles and points to a second shelf on the wicker table. "I just had this white napkin over the dish so that the sandwiches wouldn't dry out." Maya holds up the white napkin.

"I'm sure that I didn't see anything except the lemonade on that table when we walked up." Adele looks right into Maya's beautiful green eyes.

"People don't always see what is right in front of them, my dear."

Trudy and Adele exchange quizzical glances and shrug.

Maya rocks back in her chair. "So tell me what you've been up to today that makes you all look so roused."

"We went to see the fairies," Doni blurts out, "and it was really great!"

Maya gives Doni a delighted look. "How wonderful!"

"We went into the beam of light that we told you about yesterday," says Trudy.

"Yes," Adele says, butting in. "Our bodies shrunk down, and we were able to enter the tiny passageway, and then we went through a tunnel together. We held hands and just floated in."

"There's a tunnel under the tree?"

"Well, kind of," Jeff says, jumping in. "The beginning of it is by the roots of the tree, and you sort of start under the tree, but you go straight. You don't go down."

Maya sits back comfortably and takes another sip of her tea. "Well," she says, addressing everyone, "tell me what you saw."

Trudy starts; she is animated as she speaks, with her hands moving almost as quickly as she is able to talk. "Oh Maya, it was so magical!" She goes on to recount most of what happened, with the others chiming in as well. They all take turns making comments and telling amusing accounts of what happened. When Richie and Jeff tell of their meeting with Tom, everyone sits still and is especially interested, because the two boys have not related this encounter to the others.

Richie has his notebook in hand as he speaks. "Tom said that his tribe of people makes paper out of some plant from Africa. Do you know what plant he is talking about, Maya?"

"I've heard of some plant that is used for paper that does not have to be killed first, but I can't remember where it comes from. I believe that the plant name begins with the letter k, but I'm not really sure."

"I'll check the Internet tonight," Richie replies.

It seems to take longer to recount everything that happened than it did to experience it. It is midafternoon before they get to the end of their fairy tale.

"My, my." The old woman practically whispers these words; she has a dreamy, youthful look upon her face as she takes everything that they have said under consideration. She waits a few moments before saying anything. "It seems that you have a great decision to make, my dears. There are many beings waiting for your return. How do you feel about this responsibility?"

"I'm going! I want to go back," Doni announces. "It was so much fun! I want to see Topsy again." He then turns to his brother. "You want to go too, right?"

Richie nods. "I'm going."

"Me too," Jeff declares, and he puts his arm around the shoulders of his best friend. "As I see it, we have nothing to lose by going back, and maybe we can be of help."

Richie holds up his notebook. "Yeah, and what a fantastic story it will make." Then, looking back at Maya, he says," I guess I'll need to get a new one. This one is filled."

"You've recorded all of your findings?"

Richie nods.

"Why, that's wonderful, Richie. I look forward to reading your story when you've finished with all of your accounts."

Maya then gives her attention to the girls. "You're awfully quiet, darlings."

"Adele's not sure that she wants to go back." Trudy looks at Adele as she speaks, but she is looking at the side of Adele's head, because Adele will not turn her head to look back. "But I'm going back for sure. I think that it is important for us to return."

Adele won't return Trudy's gaze, nor does she speak. She is looking down at her shoes and rocking in the chair as if she is alone.

Maya puts her hand on Adele's. "This is an important decision, and maybe some thought about your return is required." She pats the hand. "I'm sure Adele will make a good decision."

"Oh gosh!" Trudy jumps up from the floor. "What time is it?"

Shading her eyes with one hand, Maya looks up to see where the sun is located. "It is close to four o'clock, Trudy. Why?"

"My parents are hosting the monthly neighborhood potluck tonight, and I told them I'd be home to help."

Everyone says good-bye and takes a turn hugging Maya; the cat and dogs quit their game of chase, and the dogs take off after their owners. Henry walks up the porch steps and stands by Maya, and the two of them watch their departing visitors disappear over the hill. Maya sits back down in her rocker and picks up her iced tea. Henry jumps back up onto the railing, stretches his back, and then lies down.

"It is a good day to die." Maya smiles as she remembers this old Native American saying, which means that it is the best day of all days. "A very good day indeed."

The potluck dinner is going well. Trudy's mom has just served the strawberry shortcake that Jeff's mom made, and all the young neighbors are gathering in the Truhardts' backyard to enjoy it.

Adele's sister, Wanda, and Jeff's little sister, Annette, are on the swings, singing silly songs, and the ten-year-old Piper twins—Melissa and Cori— are playing in the sandbox. The twins look alike but are not identical. They are the new kids on the block.

Jeff rounds up his fellow travelers as the curious twins watch; they pretend to play so that no one will know they are spying on the older group.

It is a beautiful autumn evening. Only light sweatshirts or sweaters are required to keep their bodies warm. Jeff, Richie, Adele, and Trudy are sitting at the picnic table. "Where's your brother, Richie?" Adele asks.

"He's with my dad; we don't need him right now anyway. He'll do whatever we want as long as he gets to go back."

The sky is turning a dark indigo blue. Jeff lights the bug light on the picnic table, and it gives everyone sitting there an eerie look.

"Well, I don't know about you guys, but I'm going back." Trudy whispers so that no one else can hear. The twins lean toward the table, trying to listen, and are a bit annoyed at the squeaky noise coming from the chains of the swings.

"We're all going, aren't we?" Richie makes sure everyone is nodding. "We just have to decide when and where we should meet up."

Adele leans in close. "Are we telling our parents?" The thought of not telling her mom makes her feel uneasy. What if something happens? Shouldn't their parents know?

The others look back and forth at each other until all eyes stop on Trudy. "No. Not yet. Let's make sure we know everything before we say something. They're not going to believe us anyway unless we have some kind of proof." Everyone nods in agreement.

Adele sighs and looks up at the bright autumn moon. The night sky is always beautiful this time of year. As she stares upward, she thinks she sees a twinkling star coming toward her. Then she sees more than one. The stars are Lilly and Maggie; they are tiny and quick. Adele taps Trudy on the shoulder so that she will look, and as she points to them, they disappear, giving off just a small streak of light.

Jeff turns to Adele and whispers a bit too loudly, "Was that Lilly and Maggie?"

The twins have left the sandbox and are crawling toward the table; they have heard and seen everything but do not understand it at all. Melissa looks at Cori and puts her index finger to her lips; they keep moving forward toward the picnic table.

"Hi, everybody!" Doni's voice is loud and cheerful as he comes around the side of the house. "I was looking everywhere for you." As the last word comes out of his mouth, his foot collides with Cori's back feet, and he trips over her, falling forward. He puts out his hands and lands on his palms and knees. Cori does a half roll onto her side and yelps in fear, grabbing her sister's ankle, causing her to yell out too. The group at the picnic table all stand up to help and quickly see that everyone is okay. One by one, the startled members of the gathering catch their breath and start to laugh. Doni and the twins are laughing the hardest, making it almost impossible to stand up again.

Doni finally stands up and walks over to the table where his brother is still laughing. "What's going on?"

"Well, it looks like the Piper twins were trying to sneak up on us, and you inadvertently caught them."

Everyone laughs harder and looks to the twins for confirmation on their act of spying. Both girls are embarrassed by the incident and say nothing. They just stand and brush off their clothes.

Trudy walks over to them and, pointing, says, "You're Melissa and Cori, right?"

The girls don't speak but nod. They hold hands and look frightened. Trudy looks down on them and comes right to the point: "Did you hear what we were talking about?"

Cori speaks first. "We know that you're going someplace that you don't want your parents to know about." Melissa pokes Cori with her elbow; she doesn't want her sister to say anything else. Cori rubs her side and gives Melissa an angry look.

"We don't care about where you're going." Melissa tries to sound tough; she grabs her sister's hand. "Let's go!" She pulls on Cori's hand, and the two girls start to walk away; however, Tinkerbelle and Tiny are behind them, and being the friendly dogs that they are, they start to jump up on them and lick them. Tinkerbelle licks Melissa right in the face, stopping her immediately. "Ugh, gross!" She wipes her face with her T-shirt. Cori laughs and stoops down to pet Tiny on her head; she loves dogs.

"Don't leave." Trudy puts her hand on Melissa's shoulder to turn her around. "We're not mad. We just want to know what you've heard—that's all."

Melissa takes a deep breath and lets it out as she answers. "We told you already."

"Here." Adele pats the bench she is sitting on. "Come sit with us—maybe we can use your help."

The boys exchange glances of doubt but move over so that the girls can sit with them; however, the twins don't move.

Wanda and Annette have quit swinging to watch what is happening at the picnic table. They slide off of the swings and head for the table. They too think that the dogs' greeting of the twins was pretty funny and are giggling about it and want to see more, but Jeff stops them short in their tracks. "Annette, go play," Jeff commands, pointing back to the swings. "This is a private meeting."

Wanda looks to her sister, hoping for a different response, but only gets shrugged shoulders from Adele. Not wanting to argue, the two little girls walk sadly back to the swings with the dogs happily trailing after them. As the girls walk away, Adele gives Jeff a slightly mad look to show her disapproval of the way he talked to their sisters.

"Well, we can't take the whole neighborhood back with us. Can we?" Jeff answers, a bit annoyed by the look.

"I guess not," agrees Adele, "but be nice, Jeff—try not to sound so mean."

Jeff tilts his head and gives Adele a close-lipped smile. "Sorry."

"We're not going anywhere with you guys!" Melissa and Cori put their arms around each other as a sign of unity. "We just want to know what's going on!"

Trudy feels sorry for the girls; she doesn't want them to feel afraid. "Look, if we tell you, you'll want to come. That's the problem. So maybe it would be better if you just didn't know."

"We want to know!" Melissa is adamant.

"Are you doing something bad?" Cori adds in a frightened whisper.

"Oh, no." Trudy is surprised at the suggestion. "Not bad. It's wonderful, really. I think it's the most wonderful thing that's ever happened to me."

Melissa drops her hold on Cori and steps forward. "Then why is it a secret?"

Richie puts down his notebook and slaps both of his hands on the table; he thinks that all of this is a waste of time and wants it to end so that they can get back to planning their return. He stands up, leans into Melissa's face, and loudly whispers, "Because people will think we're crazy—that's why!"

Jeff grabs Richie by the shoulder and pushes him back down onto the bench. Richie lets out a long sigh and looks over at Trudy. "Tell 'em already! We've got some decisions to make." He puts his hand to his forehead.

Melissa perks up. "We'll be quiet; we won't tell." She looks at her sister. "We promise." Both girls give the group sincere smiles and nods of promise.

Everyone sits still as Trudy repeats the events of the day with only a little help from her friends. When she finishes, Melissa and Cori are both smiling, which clues in the others that they are adding two more to their excursion tomorrow. They decide to meet behind Trudy's garage at 9:30 a.m. and agree that if someone doesn't show, it is for a good reason, and the others will continue on without him or her.

Trudy goes to bed hoping that her angel will show; she is restless with excitement and wants to see Danielle. The angel's light finally appears around midnight, and as soon as Trudy sees Danielle's smile, she falls into a deep sleep and dreams of the beautiful fairies.

Sunday mornings are usually quiet in the Truhardts' home, and today is no exception. Linda and Joe have the weekend newspaper spread out all over the kitchen table, and they are both enjoying their first cup of coffee and Linda's homemade banana bread when Trudy enters. "Morning." Trudy kisses them both on the cheek and then grabs a piece of banana bread and pours herself a glass of grape juice. She quickly gulps down the juice and heads for the back door.

"Wait a minute." Trudy's mom is peeking over the top of her newspaper. "Where are you going in such a hurry?"

"I'm meeting up with the guys."

"Where?"

"Out back." Trudy casually points toward the garage.

Joe flips down the top of his paper and looks at his daughter. "And then where are you going?"

"Around."

He peers at her over his reading glasses. "Not a good answer, Tru."

"Dad"—she drags the word out—"I'm almost fourteen years old. I'm a big girl!"

"You're my big girl. Now where are you going?" He is becoming annoyed.

"We're just going to hang out by the creek and stuff—nothing important. I won't be far away, and I'll be with Adele, Jeff, Richie, and Doni and maybe the Piper sisters."

Trudy's mom breaks in. "How nice that you're including the girls next door. How old are they anyway?"

"I think that they are around Doni's age, maybe older. I don't really know."

Linda turns to Joe. "These potluck parties are a great way for the kids to get to know one another, aren't they?"

Joe pops the newspaper back to its original position in front of his face. "You be careful, sweetie."

"Love you, Dad." Trudy starts to move toward the back door again. "Love you too, Mom."

Trudy has almost made it to the door, when her mom asks, "When will you be home, honey?"

"I'm not sure. Maybe around four." She puts her hand on the doorknob.

"What about lunch?"

Trudy walks back to the table, grabs another piece of banana bread, and wraps it in a napkin. "I'll take this with me, and if I get really hungry, I'll come home."

"Okay." Her mom flips the newspaper back up, and Trudy makes it out the back door at last.

Jumping down the back stairs, Trudy notices Jeff walking up her driveway with Doni and Richie following close behind him. "Are you ready?" Jeff yells out, rubbing his hands together in excitement. Trudy puts her index finger to her lips and nods. As they round the back of the garage, they see Adele and the twins waiting for them. Trudy is so happy to see Adele that she runs to her and gives her a huge hug.

"I guess we should get going," Richie says, waving to the others to follow him. They are all quiet as they follow the path to the old oak. They walk quickly but not fast enough for Doni. He takes off running ahead of the group, and when they catch up with him, he is running around the tree, looking for the entryway.

"I know this is the root, but I can't see the tunnel." Doni is starting to panic as he runs around the tree. "I can't see it!"

Trudy can see that Doni's panicked yell has frightened the twins. "Calm down!" she tells him. "We'll find it."

Trudy's heart sinks a bit when she doesn't see it either, so she backs up to the bush that she and Adele hid behind, and sure enough, she spots it. "It's right there, Doni." She points to the gnarled root. "See it?"

Doni brushes some of leaves out of the way, and he can see the tiny beam of light emerging from the entryway. It isn't as bright as it was, but it is still there. He turns to the twins. "You're going to shrink," he informs them, and he kicks his foot into the beam so that they can see his foot shrink. The girls back up in astonishment. "Don't worry, you guys—it doesn't hurt."

"Are you ready?" Adele speaks softly as she takes the girls' hands in hers. "Just hold on—I won't let go."

They hear the dogs rushing toward them as they take hands. "Guard the tree," Trudy tells them. "Stay here!" The dogs stop and sit down to watch. Then she turns to the others. "Ready?" They all nod and grab each other's hands. Trudy moves the rest of the leaves out of the way, and the beam shoots out in front of her. She thrusts her free hand into it and is quickly pulled into the rainbow-colored light and down into the entrance.

Trudy tries to pay more attention to what is in the tunnel this time. She sees a number of animals moving in the same direction as she, but they are walking, not flying, as she is. She can see the end of the tunnel up ahead, so she lets go of Doni's hand so that she can fly alone. It is exhilarating to move at such a high speed, twisting and turning in flight. She doesn't want to stop, but as she reaches the end of the tunnel, her feet slowly meet the ground. She turns to see if everyone is behind her and then walks out of the tunnel. Everything looks the way she remembers it, and she is relieved. They are all eager to see the looks on the twins' faces as they enter this beautiful fairyland.

"Isn't it great?" Doni exclaims as the twins walk out of the tunnel.

Melissa and Cori stand together holding hands and looking around in wide-eyed disbelief at the wonder of it all. Their legs are a bit shaky, but they look happy. They are feeling the type of excitement that people feel after they get off a fun, fabulous amusement park ride but are not sure if they'd like to try it again. Adele comes up from behind them and puts her arms around their shoulders. "It's okay," she says to comfort them. "You can go back at any time."

At that moment, Lilly appears in front of them, looking so incredibly radiant that she takes their breath away. Looking at the twins, she sings out, "Welcome! I'm so glad that you came along. My name is Lilly." She turns slightly as the others fly up. "And these are my friends." Then, pointing to each fairy, she introduces them to the girls. "This is Maggie, Blossom, Topsy, Nena, Will, and Phil."

Delighted to see Will and Phil, Cori gushes, "I didn't know that fairies could be twins! I'm so happy to meet you!"

Will takes off his cap and bows to the girls. "Everything that is great in your outer world is here in our inner world, plus much, much more." Will's lighthearted way of talking and Phil's pleasant smile put Cori and Melissa at ease.

"Well, what's next?" Jeff is in a hurry to find out just what is expected of all of them.

Nena, who is behind Jeff, answers, "We are going back to the oak tree to get the blessing from our queen and king." She slightly pushes Jeff forward. "And then we will teach you about the immortal spirits of our world so that you can use this knowledge to give you the powers you'll need to accomplish the goals that we have set for you." Nena keeps lightly pushing Jeff along the path. "We'll show you how things work together on the earth, and then you can begin to teach others." Jeff stumbles as she pushes him along. He puts his arms out in front of him in case he falls, and he turns his head from side to side, trying to see Nena as she speaks to him. The sight of the two of them is quite comical, and it makes the others laugh as they follow along.

Lilly flies up to the front of the line. "Slow down—we don't need to rush." Jeff is relieved, and when the others catch up with them, they proceed toward the oak tree at a safer pace. They don't run into anyone this time, giving everyone a chance to take in the beauty of the fairy world. Trudy keeps an eye out for the fox but sees and feels nothing. She is slightly disappointed. She really wants to see it.

A couple of gnomes are walking out of the entrance of the oak when the group arrives. Melissa is thinking how cute they look in their pointed red hats, when one of them walks over to her and hugs her. "You're cute too!" he says in a small, squeaky voice. Melissa laughs in surprise and then looks up at Phil, who is flying next to her.

"Most of the gnomes can read your unguarded thoughts when your thoughts are loving. Some of them can read all of your thoughts, which can be quite burdensome to them at times," explains Phil.

"Have a happy visit!" The gnome shakes the visitors' hands and leaves to meet up with his friend, who also waves hello.

Cori's and Melissa's eyes widen as they walk into the vestibule of the grand ballroom; there is so much to see.

"This is where the party was." Doni is pointing toward the great hall. They all walk to the three stairs leading to the ballroom and then enter.

As they descend the stairs, they hear a soft, strong voice say, "Come. Welcome!" Looking up toward the throne area, they see the figures of the king and queen standing there.

"That's them!" Doni whispers excitedly to Cori and Melissa. "The king and queen of fairyland!"

The fairies fly directly to the throne area and bow to the royal couple; they then present their guests, making sure to introduce Melissa and Cori first.

The king looks at Trudy and smiles and then says to everyone, "Welcome back. We are most pleased to see all of you here again and happy that you brought along your young friends."

Cori's and Melissa's hearts are pumping quickly—not because they are afraid but because they are excited to be here.

The queen rises and, looking upward, raises her hands into the air with her palms held high and says, "May the immortal influence shine through all of you as you attempt this important work."

The king then places his hand on the forehead of each new student, starting with Trudy, and says, "Listen to the voice within you, and do not hesitate to act in love at all times." He steps back to the throne and stands with the queen to continue. "There will be moments when loving yourself and others will be difficult—not because you are unworthy but because there is much negativity on our earth. Negativity is a disease of the soul; it spreads swiftly, and it is hard to get rid of. There is only one weapon we can use against it correctly, and that weapon is love—pure love. Pure and honest love will kill negativity. We have invited you here to learn how to connect with the power of love that is in each of you and to use it to conquer the forces of negativity. We will show you how to embrace and hold on to your power. If you work hard, you will see your connection with the immortal influence, the All of the universe, and no one will be able to stop your mastery of this power—except, of course, yourself."

As the king speaks, Trudy can feel her chest expanding with excitement. She knows these words are true, even though she doesn't understand the whole meaning behind them yet. She wants to do what the king and queen are asking of her, but at the same time, she doesn't feel that she can; she is experiencing a weird flood of feelings. Her strongest desire is to accomplish what is being asked of her. She looks around at the others and can see that they are experiencing the same things. She also notices that the great hall is filling up with many of the residents of the inner world. She starts to get a feeling of strength building up inside of her; the more beings that enter the hall, the more strength she can feel gathering inside of her. It is as if all of the beings are giving her some of their energy, sharing their love and concern.

Trudy looks straight into the eyes of the queen. "Why are you so concerned with the outer world? When I look around this room and see all of the happy faces, I am confused as to why you want to help the outer world. Your world is fine."

The queen walks over to Trudy and takes her hand in both of hers; Dancing Waters is small and dainty, with tiny hands, but her lovely, soft voice is regal, and it is the only sound that can be heard when she speaks. "We are the caretakers of the earth, which means that we must work in the outer world with you, and it is becoming more and more difficult for us to do the work required of us because of the negativity there. Our workers are being severely affected by all of this negativity. We are starting to see these adverse traits in our craftspeople, some of whom are known for their playful pranks and mischievous tricks, and this cannot be. We do not want to see them become more than lighthearted pranks. I am speaking about the influence of humans who refuse to take action toward caring for our Earth Mother. We are seeing beings that only care about the self in every moment of their existence. They love only themselves; they do not love others or our precious earth. They are greedy for only the one moment of feeling good, and then they move on to experience the next moment of feeling. Between these moments of fleeting feelings, they undergo the fear of not having. This fear happens because they are only experiencing the feeling of the love that they have for themselves. They are not concerned for others. There is no love exchanged with other beings in their actions; therefore, it is an empty, momentary feeling. There must be an exchange of love in all actions in order for beings to feel complete. Love cannot come to you if you are not giving love out. It is how the universe works."

Richie, who is writing all of this down in his new notebook, interrupts the queen. "I don't understand how this is infecting your world. If you are all working in love, then how can that change your inhabitants in a negative way?"

The queen responds with an example. "Try to see the earth as a new baby—it is pure love. The baby is a clean slate; it will react from its experiences to form its thoughts and the way it responds. In a welcoming family, the baby does not work at anything to receive love; love comes to it freely even though it is extra work for the family. This work is happy because everyone feels the pure love of this being, and they welcome the extra work as a sign of family strength. But how about the family that sees the baby as difficult work? They may have wanted the baby but not the work involved, just as some may want to live on a beautiful, clean earth but do not want to work at keeping it clean. The baby is still pure love; however, it is looked at differently. The baby is looked at as a problem to be solved by the family. It is much harder to love something that is seen as hard work or a problem. Love itself becomes the work, and if the work is thought of as hard, then it becomes a burden. Less energy is given to the baby, and more energy is given to the work, making this innocent being a cause for anxiety instead of a cause for joy. Resentment then builds, and it slowly becomes a negative situation; the negativity then spreads through the family and, eventually, out into the world, until having a family feels like an obligation instead of a gift. There is little joy left in the care of the family. This is a simplified way to look at the earth, but it is important to see it as pure love and not a burden to be solved. We are all part of the family of Earth; we should be joyous in our work to keep her clean and happy. It should not be looked at as a burden but as a privilege. There is too much negativity surrounding our love for Mother Earth, and it is infecting all of us. We need to change the way that we see things. We need to look at everything through the eyes of love. We can no longer ignore her cries. She needs us all to care for her. We are a family and must work as one—not in separate little ways, but together. Even when we work by ourselves, we should show our love of Earth and her citizens, as a family member would. The concern for self must reach out as a concern for all. We, the fairy kingdom, feel that we should work as a family with all the inhabitants of Earth instead of in our separate ways, and that is why we want to teach you what we know. Together we are the family of Earth."

The king walks over to where his queen is standing and puts his arm around her. Then, looking up at Trudy, he says, "We will teach you the magic of Earth. Our hope is that you will then take this power with you and teach others."

The queen looks to her king with a deep, abiding love and then looks at the gathering before them. The couple puts their arms up with their palms facing the crowd, and together they say, "Our blessings and love to all of you!"

Then the king adds, "We will all do our best to help these courageous souls in understanding the power that they hold. We will do it for the All!"

Everyone cheers. Celestial sparks shoot out around them.

14

The fairies are taking turns congratulating and encouraging their recruits, along with the rest of the assembly, when Dancing Waters asks Lilly, "Where were you thinking of taking them first?"

"I thought that we should let Tom or Ansel show our friends more of our environment. I want to show them what the earth once looked like; I think it will make an important impact on them and encourage their decision to teach others."

"And also help them get an idea of what the entire planet will be losing if we don't connect on some level with one another," Phil adds.

Gentle Mountain Lion gathers the group together and starts them walking toward the direction of the gardens. "Come, we'll walk with you and look for those two elves. They're usually in the garden work shed or the surrounding area."

The crowd parts as the royal couple and their entourage walk to the entrance of the gardens. Everyone they pass smiles and greets them with encouraging words of welcome. The great hall is filled with happiness and hope. Trudy can feel the love that is being shown to them and can't contain her giggles as they follow their leaders out of the great hall to the garden entry door.

When they reach the entry, the king pushes the beautifully carved oak door open. Everyone gasps at the sights that lie before them; never have any of them seen a garden of such extraordinary beauty!

"Oh my goodness!" whispers Adele. "This is the loveliest place I've ever seen!" The twins are standing on either side of her, holding her hands. They both look up at her and then back at the picturesque garden that lies before them. They hardly breathe, afraid that it isn't real and will all disappear in the blink of an eye. Even the boys are struck by its elegance and charm. Richie has stopped writing; his notebook and pencil fall to the ground as he takes in the sight. The clear blue of the sky and the expanse of land and mountains framing the garden create a magnificent landscape. The pathway they take from the passageway to the oak tree is certainly beautiful but is nothing like this!

Blossom flies up to the front of the group. "All of Earth once looked like this. This is how it looked at its beginning and how it could look again. It will take hard work, but we can do it!" Her wings are fluttering as she speaks, and little gold flecks of love are sprinkling around her, making her look even more glorious.

"Isn't she a beauty?" Jamie softly says into Richie's ear.

Richie jumps back a little, startled by hearing Jamie. "When did you get here?"

"I'm your muse; I'm always around. You just don't notice me all the time, because I'm so small. But whenever you're writing or thinking creatively, I'm around! Better pick up your notebook and pencil; soon you'll have plenty to write about." Jamie is right in front of Richie's face, smiling, causing Richie to laugh out loud.

"Has anyone seen Ansel or Tom yet?" Lilly says as she looks around the garden.

"Ansel is in here!" Topsy's squeaky little voice rings out. He is floating over the giant lilies of the valley and pointing down at what appears to be a work area.

Ansel looks up from his workbench and claps the dirt from his hands. "Hi, Topsy! Whatcha up to this grand morning?"

"They've come back, and they're ready to learn! Come on out and say hello."

Ansel walks out through the lilies of the valley to the stone walkway. "Good day!" he says, bowing to the royal couple and their friends. "It's grand to see that you've all returned." And then, noticing the twins, he says, "And you've brought some more friends with you." He bows slightly to Cori and then Melissa, making them smile.

"The garden has never looked more beautiful, Ansel!" the queen says. "Thank you!" She smiles at the little, skinny elf.

"It's truly my pleasure." Ansel smiles back.

The king then addresses the group: "We leave you in good hands. Learn all that you can, and have fun. We will join you later." Still holding his queen's hand, he turns, and they walk back through the oak door and close it behind them.

Ansel waves his hands to shoo the fairies. "You can all go about your work now and catch up with us later. We'll be fine."

"Are you sure you won't need us?" Will politely asks.

"I want to stay!" Topsy whines.

Ansel brushes the top of Topsy's head. "You all have good work to do. Your friends will be fine with me."

Reluctantly, the fairies say their good-byes and go their separate ways.

"We'll be back later," Nena cries out as she flies away.

Richie's eyes search for Jamie. He is curious to see if Jamie has gone with the others. "I'm still here," he hears Jamie whisper. "I'm always with you!"

Ansel also takes notice of Jamie and nods. "Creativity is always welcome," he says, and then he quickly scans his group of students. "Let's take a walk." They follow the elf along the stone path to the outside garden gate. The gate and surrounding fence are made of bent branches and vines. The construction is welcoming. It certainly is not built to keep anyone out. The vines have delicious-looking grapes growing from them, and Ansel offers the group some of the fruit as they walk through the gate to the open expanse on the other side. They walk out to the cliff, the same spot where Ansel sat with Tom the day before. When all are assembled, Ansel swings his arms out in front of himself and says, "This is our world!" He gives everyone a moment to soak in his words and the view. "Your outer world looked the same at one time. With love and hard work, it will look this way again. My friends and I will teach you, and you will teach your people."

No one speaks; they do not have words for how they feel at this moment. What lies before them is majestic. The soft green valleys are loaded with color, the mighty mountains are strong and protective, and the heavenly blue sky with its puffy white clouds is so clear. Then there are the birds—oh, the birds. Their lovely song of peace is everywhere, harmonizing with the music that is always around. There are butterflies of every shape and color, dragonflies and pretty blue damselflies, and bumblebees swerving in and out of the giant flowers and grasses. The bees make a hum like a bass guitar. Glorious animals dot the landscape, some in herds and some alone. Every movement, every sound, is like a perfect melody. They can hear the trickle of creeks and waterfalls. All is connected, all has purpose, and all shows love. It is encompassing. Each spectator feels a part of this symphony when gazing down upon it. It is an explosion of love for all things of the earth; there is no feeling of entitlement or of dominance—just raw, unconcealed emotion. Each beholder feels the passion of the harmony of life and the force that connects them with the All of the universe.

Ansel can see the recognition of their relationships with Mother Earth materializing on their faces; he sees that their bodies are rocking rhythmically back and forth as they each connect with the natural sounds of the earth. His students are just beginning to understand what their mission is. They are not just living on the earth; they are, in fact, part of it! Ansel wants them to know that everything works together in a beautiful way. They are not singular entities working alone and taking care of just the self. Each is a working part of the lyrical expression of the All that is Earth and the universe.

The group stands on the cliff that is their overlook, and they put their arms around each other, each silently looking into the eyes of the other, receiving and giving strength for their mission and passing along the love that runs through them from one to the other. The soft breeze whispers a song of triumph, giving them the courage to say yes.

"Look!" An excited voice comes from behind them. "Up there!" The distinct voice comes from Tom, and he is pointing upward as he walks around the group to the cliff's edge. "She's back!"

Everyone looks skyward in the direction that Tom is pointing; it takes a moment for their eyes to adjust. Then they all see the reddish thing with wings that he is excited about. But what is it?

Ansel is happy to see his friend and follows him to the cliff's edge. "Ahhh, she is lovely, isn't she?" he says as he puts his arm around Tom's shoulder.

"It's a good omen, Ansel!" Tom is delighted to see the red dragon again.

The children hear Tom's words but are not sure what he is talking about when he mentions the omen; their attention has shifted to the thing in the sky that he called the red dragon. They are dumbfounded by the sight. A dragon is flying right above them! It is a dark brownish red with large, bat-like purple wings, and it looks just like the pictures of the Mexican dragons they've all seen before in the Mayan myth and legend stories from school.

"Wow!" the boys gush in unison.

"She's huge!" Jeff can't take his eyes off of her.

The twins are trying to hide behind Adele. "Do you think she'll hurt us?" Melissa panicks. Adele looks around at the faces of the others for an answer, but no one complies. She has no answer for them either, so she stands still and watches with the others as the twins push to hide behind her.

While Trudy watches the dragon, she thinks about the Native America story that Maya once told her about the thunderbird and wonders if this is the creature in the story. As she watches it, she notices that it is not flying quickly at all but seems to be just floating lazily among the soft, billowy clouds as she comes closer to the cliff where they all are standing. The dragon is descending slowly; she is coming straight down now and seems interested in the group that is staring up at her. As she comes in for a closer look, the watchers back away, all except Trudy.

"Stop!" yells out Tom. "She won't hurt you—stay still."

They do as they are told. The dragon comes in close and sniffs at them. She looks like she is smiling, so Trudy smiles back at her. The dragon's head is as big as the coffee table her parents have in the family room. Her eyes are a strange green-gray color, and her brownish elephant-like skin has small reddish-orange hairs all over it. This huge animal does not scare Trudy at all; on the contrary, she is delighted to see it. She puts her hand up as the dragon comes down in front of her, and she slowly moves it toward the dragon's snout, trying to touch her. The dragon moves a tiny bit closer. Trudy stands on the edge of the cliff and pats the dragon on the nose while everyone gasps in surprise. The creature opens her mouth in the pleasure of being petted; shows her giant, sharp teeth; and gives everybody a whiff of her smoky, sweet breath. As her wings flap back and forth, they give off a slight musical sound kind of like a large harp; it is beautiful. It is both scary and wonderful. The dragon slowly retreats and starts to ascend skyward. Her wings push a gush of wind toward the bystanders, making it difficult for them to stand still. They watch this incredible animal until she becomes a tiny dot in the sky. No one speaks right away. Trudy still has her arm stretched out in front of her with her hand extended.

Richie has his notebook in hand, and breaking the silence, he says softly, "What did she feel like, Tru?"

Trudy pulls her hand in toward her face and stares at it for a moment; then she lets out a big sigh as she turns to answer Richie. "Her skin was rough, but the tiny hairs were soft." She then puts her hand by her nose and adds, "She had a sweet smell."

Doni, the twins, and Adele sit down on the grass and are too stunned to talk. Jeff sits down next to them, feeling as if all the air inside of him has been kicked out. Ansel and Tom are staring at Trudy in amazement. They have never seen a dragon this close up, let alone seen anyone touch one.

Tom looks up into Trudy's thoughtful face. "You are truly magical!" This statement comes as a surprise to everyone, even Trudy. She looks back at her friends, who are staring at her in awe and can say nothing; she then sits down at the edge of the cliff with everyone else and becomes lost in her own thoughts. Everyone stays quiet for what seems to be a long time. No one knows what to say. Even the elves are stunned by what they have seen, and they need a moment to collect themselves before moving on.

"You were right about this being a good omen," Tom whispers to Ansel. "The girl Trudy has great magic!"

"I believe that they all do."

15

"We should get moving." Ansel is standing in front of the group with Tom at his side.

Richie stands up, brushing off the back of his jeans. "Where are we going?"

"I'm hungry," Doni says in a sleepy voice.

Ansel gives Doni a fatherly look and then addresses everyone. "We'll go get something to eat, and then we'll go visit some of our wise ones. Let's get a move on!"

"Will we see that dragon again?" Melissa's small voice is a bit shaky.

Tom walks up to her and pats her on the back. "Not to worry, little one. The dragon is not mean. She will not harm the innocent, and I do hope we see her again."

"I do too!" exclaims Doni.

"I didn't even think that dragons really existed," says Richie. "I thought they were just in legends and storybooks—you know, mythical things like ..." Richie stops talking and looks at Ansel.

"You mean like fairies and elves?" Ansel laughs.

Richie blushes and nods. Everyone giggles.

"There are many beings here that lived in the outer world at one time or another but now live here exclusively. When we notice that there are animals in danger of extinction on our earth, we try to convince them to come here and live. Some come; however, there are those that do not come. They choose to live and die in the outer world. It is what they wish."

"Are you saying that mythical creatures are not mythical but actually lived with us?" Adele asks.

"Some. And some are products of a writer's imagination, of course," Tom says as the group starts out on their trek.

Melissa takes Tom's hand as they walk, leaving Cori with Adele. "Did all the dragons look like that one? Were they all that big?" she asks.

"Oh no." Tom shakes his head. "The red dragons are the biggest of all the dragons that we have here. There are also green dragons, which are about as big as a horse, and the now-extinct golden dragons, which were more snakelike and about as large as an alligator but a bit longer."

"Were they really made of gold?" This notion has sparked Melissa's imagination.

"No. Their skin was a yellowish color, hence their name. They were considered good luck in ancient times, and every king on Earth wanted one in his court and would pay a high price to have one. They did not survive well in captivity. They needed to fly in order to keep up their good health, so a cage was not a very good home, no matter how large it was. They also needed to be by water because that is where they came from. They lived in caves deep in the seas, and they breathed a golden mist instead of fire. Some of our people believe that the fairy world was created in the mist of the golden dragon. Humans believed that the caves of all the dragons were rich in treasure, and that is another reason that they did not endure; it is a shame on all of us that these gentle creatures did not survive. It was after the complete demise of the golden dragon that our people decided to try to save the outer-world animals should they become endangered on our earth, and we've done a pretty good job of it. The unicorn was one of our best saves; there are many that live here, and we are now working on trying to save the polar bears. In all, we are working on trying to save about twenty species."

"Polar bear cubs are so cute—I love them!" Cori says. "I'd hate to see them die."

Jeff wants to know more about the dragons, so he decides to steer the conversation back to them. "So the green dragons are still around?"

"Yes. However, I've never seen one for myself. They are extremely timid, preferring to stay in large caves. Their wings are much smaller than those of the red dragon, so they don't fly far from their lair. We honor their desire to be left alone, so I do not know that much about them. We can try to find someone who does when we return, if you like."

"You said that the red dragon was the biggest that you have living here. Are there larger dragons somewhere else?"

"The Native Americans have a story about the creation of the earth that includes a very large dragon with horns, but I have never seen it. This dragon was said to have helped in the making of the mountains and even some islands."

"I didn't know that there were dragons in the Americas!" Cori says excitedly. "That's so cool!"

"Most cultures have stories about dragons. The beings on this planet are more alike than different; you can see this in the folk tales that are told around the world."

Richie is writing this all down as he walks, and he is curious about how many dragons could be flying about. "Do you think that we will see more of them?"

"Seeing a dragon is an extremely rare occurrence, even for us," Tom explains. "To have seen one fly up to a group like us is unheard of."

"Is that why you said that Trudy was magical, Tom?" Adele asks.

"Partly, but I believe that all of Earth's children are born magical; they just aren't taught how to use their powers, so they lose them."

The children all look at each other and smile about the idea that someone thinks they are each magical.

"The orchard is right around the bend here." Ansel points ahead toward the curve in the road.

"What is that wonderful smell?" Trudy runs ahead of the others, with Doni right on her heels. As they round the corner, they are both taken aback at the sight they behold. Hundreds of giant fruit trees of all kinds stand before them, ripe with delicious offerings. The sweet smell is captivating. Trudy and Doni are standing at the edge of the orchard, staring at the magnificent sight before them, when the others catch up with them. The smell is too overwhelming for Doni, and he starts to run for what looks like an apple tree.

"Wait!" yells Tom.

"Stop!" Ansel cries out as he runs after Doni. "You must ask first!"

Doni stops and turns to look at Ansel. "Okay, can I have some fruit?" he says, puzzled by their insistence.

Ansel smiles. "You need not ask us. You need to ask the trees."

Tom notices how confused they all look as he walks toward the cherry tree that Doni is standing next to, and he says, "Thank you for such beautiful cherries. May I have one?" As he speaks these words, he pulls down one of the giant cherries, which looks much larger than an apple in his small hands, and hands it to Doni.

"Do the trees talk back?" Doni whispers to Tom.

Tom talks loudly enough for all to hear. "They cannot talk in the way that you can hear, but your gratefulness and good feelings are fed into the tree so that it will continue to grow the sweet-tasting fruit."

Doni bites into the giant cherry, thinking it is an apple. "Whoa!" He is totally surprised by the taste. "This is the biggest and best cherry I've ever had!"

"It is good to remember the importance of honoring all living things," says Ansel, "but if you do not wish to speak to the tree, you may pat its trunk with your love or even hug it before taking its fruit. It is the grateful feeling that is important, not the words. Everything done in love is much sweeter."

At first, they all feel kind of funny talking to the trees, but they soon get over that feeling. They begin to understand how important it is to give the trees their love in return for this wonderful fruit. They all sit down in the soft orchard grass and eat their fill.

Trudy lies back, relaxed, with her arms behind her head, staring up at the billowy clouds. "Love is everything. Right, Ansel?"

"Yes."

"It seems so simple. Give love out, and get love back."

"In many ways, it is simple, Trudy, but it can also be complicated for those with little understanding. Trees and plants do not have emotions as we do; they love all of the time, and when they do not receive love back, they do not grow as well or produce as much fruit or flowers as they should. Their taste and fragrance suffer also. The environment that they grow in is of extreme importance; these factors are just as important as the dirt, sun, and rain. This is a fact that only a few outer-world inhabitants understand; this is the essence of what you must make your people understand and act on. Love is everything! It is the All. It is in every part of the earth and the universe beyond. Fear is the enemy. When one feels fearful, there is less love present. The more fear attached to people, the less love they can feel and, subsequently, the less love they can put into the beings and things around them. Fear pushes love away. This sounds so simple, but on our earth, fear grows rampant in the outer world, making it extremely hard to show love."

"But sometimes it's okay to be afraid," says Cori. "Isn't it?"

Tom takes her hand but speaks to everyone. "It is okay to be cautious and thoughtful and to walk away from something that is not good for you. You should not be around people that make you feel bad or unhappy in any way, shape, or form. You should leave places that threaten your safety and fight if someone tries to harm you or others that you care for, but don't stay afraid of them. You should stand up to the bad people in your world. Be stronger than they are in your actions. There are many forms that fear comes in: distrust, disappointment, anger, teasing, despair, greed, worry, unhappiness, annoyance, impatience, hatred—I could go on and on, but I think you understand my point."

"I get it," says Jeff, "but aren't those feelings part of who people are? How do you get rid of your natural emotions?"

"You don't get rid of your emotions, Jeff; you must try to act them out in love instead of acting them out in fear. It is in your actions that you can choose to feel love or fear. Fight against your fears; do not keep them with you. Do not let your fears drag you down; do not make them more important than love. The feelings of fear and the feelings of love can both draw people together, but when it is in fear that people gather, the fruit of their labors will be small and tasteless, while those that gather in love will bear fruit that is big and sweet."

Ansel stands to speak. "We know that you all come from strong, loving families. We know that you do not doubt the love that flows through all of you to each other, and that is why we know that you will do your job of teaching others with a strong conviction. This is why we believe in all of you. This is how we know that you are the right people for the job. You will act on the feelings of love because the love you have for each other is strong." He then looks at the twins. "Even though you are new to this group, you are not new to us. We've seen the love you have for each other spill out to others, and we are overjoyed that you have joined this group and have agreed to help. The small fears that you all now have will grow smaller as you understand this mission of love that we will lay before you."

Doni interrupts, "What's that noise?"

Everyone's attention is drawn to the sound of small, tinkling bells.

"Oh," says Tom, "it's the workers coming to the orchard."

Looking up in the direction of the sound, they can see hundreds of fairies flying toward the fruit trees. It is a lovely sight! There are tiny flecks of gold raining everywhere. It looks as if they are flying in a rainbow of brilliant color. As the fairies approach the trees, they touch each leaf and each piece of fruit with their love. Out of the roots of the trees march the gnomes. They hug the trunk of each tree and then pick up any fallen fruit and put it in the baskets that they are carrying. The workers smile and wave greetings, but no words are exchanged. The workers touch every blade of grass, every flower, and every leaf and fruit, and then—poof—they are all gone, and it is over. All they can hear for a second or two is the tinkling of bells.

Trudy and her friends stand in awe; their mouths are slightly open, and they are gaping at the aftermath of what they have just seen. It happened so quickly. Ansel and Tom can't help but smile; they understand how surprised the children must have been to see how the inner world put love into action.

Richie, notebook in hand, is recording the entire incident, and he can't help but smile as he writes. He is feeling pleased by what he sees, and he hopes that the words he uses to describe it will somehow show the pleasure he feels inside of himself.

"That was the most beautiful sight I've ever seen!" Adele gushes.

"It is a beautiful sight," Ansel agrees.

Tom is delighted that his group has had a chance to see something of such value. He hopes that this event will stay with them and that their excitement about it will spill over when teaching other human beings about the meaning of using love at every level in their lives. He walks over to where Doni stands and reaches up to put his hand on Doni's shoulder. "Are you ready to move on? Did you get enough to eat?"

Doni wipes his mouth with the sleeve of his shirt. "This was the best cherry that I ever ate! I hope that we can have some more later."

"Yes, of course. Are you ready to leave?"

"Yeah, I can't wait to see what else you're going to show us. This is the best day ever!"

"Come, everybody," Tom shouts out. "Let's get a move on."

No one really wants to leave the orchard; it is so peaceful. The fresh smells of the earth surround them in a safe, secure embrace that is hard to leave. Slowly, each student stands and stretches and reluctantly follows the guides out of the orchard.

16

Trudy can't shake the feeling that they are being followed by the fox; even when she is relaxing in the orchard, she feels that it is somewhere around her. Why is it following her, and why don't the others feel its presence? She walks alone for a while, her eyes searching the changing landscape for her fox, and her mind on the *why*.

As they walk, the scenery around them takes on the look of the great Southwest. The dried-mud path beneath their feet begins to look dusty, with a reddish color. The large plants that always seem to surround them become less dense as cactus plants and tumbleweeds creep into view. Huge red rocks jut out of the ground, and the mountains become more visible. The clear blue of the sky is much more intense, making the few puffy white clouds floating above them stand out in a way that makes the travelers feel as though they can touch them.

Adele is holding hands with the twins as they walk, and occasionally, she looks over her shoulder to see if Trudy is keeping up with the rest of them. Noticing the pensive look on her friend's face, Adele becomes concerned and decides to have a talk with her. The twins let go of Adele's hands as she kisses each one of them on the forehead and says, "Why don't you two walk up ahead with Tom and Jeff? I need to talk with Trudy." Adele then stops walking until Trudy catches up with her. "What's going on, Tru?"

Trudy does not stop walking but takes her friend's hand as she speaks. "I can't stop thinking about that fox, Adele. I still feel like it's following us around for some reason, and I want to know why."

"Are you afraid?"

Trudy watches as a tumbleweed rolls across their path before she answers. "No. Not really. I just want to know why it's following us, and I want it to stop."

"I haven't seen it, Tru. Are you sure it's the same fox? Maybe there are a lot of them around here and you're just mistaking them for the same fox." Their pace becomes much more deliberate, and it slows as the conversation intensifies.

Ansel notices that Trudy and Adele have dropped back from the group and look to be brooding over something. He stops so that they will catch up with him. "Can I help you with something? You look troubled."

"Well, maybe you can help," answers Trudy. "On the day that I showed Adele the green fog that came from the passageway in the oak tree, we saw a fox. The fox jumped out of the root of the tree and stared at me as if she knew me, and I believe that she's been following me around ever since—at least I feel like she's been following me."

"Trudy says she can feel the fox following us right now," says Adele, "but I haven't seen it."

Trudy stops walking so that she can look into Ansel's face to see his reaction. "I haven't seen it either. I can just feel it! I know it's around here somewhere!"

Ansel does not seem surprised to hear this. "Foxes come through here all the time, especially during the equinox. They are the guides for the seekers of the fairy world. The fox you are concerned about is probably just keeping an eye on our group because she showed you the way to enter." Ansel stops talking for a moment and looks around for the creature. "Or maybe the fox is your totem and is watching out for you. In either case, the fox should not be feared." He keeps looking.

"Totem?" questions Adele.

"Yes." Ansel starts walking faster to catch up with the others, hoping that Adele and Trudy will follow. They do. "A totem is kind of like your guardian angel, Trudy. It is an animal that helps guide you and keep you on your chosen path of learning. It is an animal that you can also learn from if you study all of its characteristics. Some societies pay tribute to the fox for bringing the gift of fire to mankind; others believe that it is a healer. Maybe she is around us now because we are trying to teach you, and because she brings fire, she can help enlighten us about healing Mother Earth. But whatever her reason is for following you, it is not to harm you or any of us."

"I guess that makes me feel a little better, but I wish I knew for sure why she was following me."

"It will let you know. Keep an open mind."

The three of them walk together in silence.

The path they have been walking on is getting smaller in width, and the background music has changed. The music is even softer than before but has a more enchanting melody. The sound is from a single wooden flute; it is light and airy in the style of the ancient Native Americans.

Tom is walking up ahead of the group, with Jeff by his side; the twins follow close behind. Richie is in the middle with his brother, Doni. Ansel, Trudy, and Adele are bringing up the rear.

"Where are you taking us, Tom?" Jeff asks.

"We are going to introduce you to one of our greatest shamans. Our hope is that you will gain a deeper knowledge of your mission by meeting some of our wise ones."

Doni is listening and runs up to Tom. "What's a shaman?"

"A shaman is a person of great knowledge," explains Tom. "They have a superior kinship with Mother Earth, and they understand her connection with humanity. Shamans are the go-betweens. They can help us feel Mother Earth's love, and they help our mother thrive under the pressures of stress."

"Stress?" Jeff doesn't like or understand this term. He has heard his mom and dad use it to explain why they can't go to his ball games or have his friends over to play. They need to spend time alone to destress from work. To Jeff, it seems as if they say this all of the time, so there is no time left for his sister or him to be with their parents.

"What kind of stress is the earth having?" asks Doni.

"The stress of being taken for granted. The stress of people taking all that they want from her without any regard, without giving anything back—not even a prayer of thanks."

"Oh." Doni's voice is sad.

"Are shamans fairies?" Cori asks.

"No, but they are part of our fairy folk that live here. They live in both worlds, although more and more of them are staying in this world. It has become harder for them to accomplish their purpose in the outer world, because fewer people have faith in their teachings now. Faith is the essence of love, and without it, they cannot do their work."

"Faith is a belief, right?"

"Yes. It is a strong belief," answers Tom.

"Is that why, in the story of Peter Pan, they save Tinker Bell by clapping hands?" Melissa asks. "Is it because they have faith?"

Tom chuckles a bit at this analogy. "Why, yes! That's exactly why."

Melissa feels happy that she understands what Tom is talking about and can explain it to the rest of her group. It is an uplifting experience for her. Tom pats her on the back as the group continues on its journey.

"Can we see the shamans when they are in the outer world?" Richie asks.

"Some of them can be seen as virtuous people living among you; however, most of them are not visible in the way that you'd expect," answers Tom.

"How do you mean?"

"This is very difficult to understand, but I will share their secret with you. Shamans are different from any other earthly species in that they have the ability to change from one species into another species in order to conceal their identity. The ancients called them shape-shifters."

Trudy and Adele become interested in this conversation and do their best to catch up to the group in order to hear.

"What kind of shapes do they turn into?" asks Adele.

"They can turn into most anything: an animal, rock, plant, or human. Whatever they choose becomes their disguise, but since all things on the planet are suffering, most choose not to conceal themselves any longer in the outer world. They choose to work from here instead, avoiding the outer world altogether."

"Wow! That's really magical!" Doni says. "Can we meet one?"

"Yes. We are on our way to meet one now," explains Ansel. "But I should also tell you that all humans are shape-shifters. Their magic works in a different way than with shamans. As I explained, shamans choose the way that others see them, but humans do not have the ability to choose how others see them. Each human sees the other only through his or her own personal experience. You see yourself one way, but others may see you differently."

"I don't get it," Adele says.

"It is a very difficult concept to understand, so I will do my best to make it clear to you. You believe yourself to be one way, and you go along in life feeling that this one way is what you are projecting to others. You are not aware of the idea that others can see you differently than the way that you see yourself. This is the cause of many heartaches and much sadness. Others see you with only their own experience. It cannot be helped; it is the way of humans. You do not know how another is seeing you. You may have a wonderful intention, but another may see it as a mistake or, worse, a deliberate meanness. This is the main cause for the negativity on your side."

"I still don't get it."

"Let me try an example to help clarify. I will aim to make it simple. Let us say that you, Adele, are babysitting for Jeff's sister, Annette, while Jeff is out with his parents. And for the sake of an example, say that Annette has had some very bad experiences with babysitters yelling at her, and this is the first time that you are watching her. We'll say that you have been told by other families that you are a wonderful sitter, so you also believe that you are a wonderful and skilled babysitter. Jeff's parents tell you that Annette is to be in bed by nine o'clock, but Annette does not want to go. You see yourself as a responsible babysitter, so you first try a stern voice and announce to Annette that it is bedtime, but she does not want to go and begins to beg for more time. You then explain to her that her parents left you in charge and that she should go to bed now. Annette still does not move from her position, which leaves you feeling ignored, so you try another tactic. You close the book that she is looking at, and in a louder voice, you tell her again to go to bed. Unexpectedly, Annette begins to cry and announces to you that you are a mean person and that she does not like you, but she goes to bed. You feel bad, and she feels bad, and both of you are acting out of past experience. You see yourself as a responsible babysitter that had to do what you did in order to follow directions. Annette sees you as another yelling babysitter, even though that was not your intention. You believe that your shape is the person that you feel you are projecting; however, the shape that Annette sees is not at all what you feel that you are projecting. In her eyes, you are just another yelling babysitter.

"What people see is shaped by their personal past experiences, and they believe what they see, so you must always be aware of what you are projecting, because your shape is always shifting from person to person. The wonderful babysitter that others may see you as is not the shape that Annette sees. This is what is meant by shape-shifting with humans, but you can occasionally control it if you understand how to use it. It can work as magic if you are aware of how others will see you. Some will see you as good, while others will see you as not so good, and some will not see you at all. That is why most teachers will tell you not to sit in judgment of others— because observing the world is a unique experience. We can only catch a glimpse of others' actions. We cannot feel the degree of their emotion or see what they are actually seeing. This is a very complex notion to grasp, but a very important one."

Richie is quickly writing down what Ansel is saying and wants to make sure he is getting the right meaning when he addresses the elf. "So you're saying that shamans have control over how you may see them, but humans only have a limited control. And you're also saying that humans cannot turn into animals, but shamans can. Is that right?"

"Exactly!" Ansel is pleased with himself.

Doni taps his brother on the shoulder. "Don't forget to say that it's magic, Richie."

"Okay." Richie slaps his brother on the back. "As long as you always see me as the magical older brother who always knows best!"

"You wouldn't say that if you could see you through my eyes!" Doni quips.

Both boys laugh and then push each other on the back of the head as they continue to follow Tom.

There isn't much vegetation around, but there are plenty of boulders and a lot of sand on the now-rocky path. The sun is bearing down on them, but they hardly feel it. The temperature does not increase more than a few degrees as they walk. Sand dunes become visible, but they seem miles away from where the travelers are.

Jeff is staring upward toward the mountains and the surrounding area, when he notices something over the top of one of the giant boulders not far away. It is a huge owl with its wings outstretched, but it isn't moving. It takes him a minute to realize that he is looking at the top of a totem pole. "Look, guys!" he yells out, pointing to the owl carving. "It's a totem pole!"

Everyone looks to where Jeff is pointing.

"Wow, it's gigantic!" shrieks Doni.

Ansel smiles at both of them. "That means we're here."

Melissa starts to walk faster. "Are we going to see that?" she says, trying to run past the front of the group.

Tom grabs her hand. "Let's all stay together."

They soon reach the boulder. On the other side of it is an immense clearing. Guarding the entrance to the clearing is a large, majestic carving of a moose. The group walks under its huge antlers to enter, and in front of them stands the totem pole with the owl on top. The owl looks as if it is landing on the wolf below it, the talons resting on the wolf's shoulders. The wolf has all of its teeth fully exposed and its mouth slightly open as it stands on the back of a grizzly bear. The grizzly's head is looking down with piercing black eyes, and its monstrous paws are standing on the back of the great American bison that stands proud at the bottom of this amazing totem pole.

A short distance behind the totem pole is a small wooden lodge. The lodge has some interesting decorations adorning it. Hanging over what appears to be the doorway is a magnificent hand-woven blanket. The same animals that are carved into the totem pole are weaved into the blanket, along with the faces of other North American animals. Over the top of the door is a realistic carving of a fox head. The fox is looking skyward and has a regal look about it. There are handmade tools hanging on exquisitely carved hooks along the outside walls of the lodge. Each tool is a work of art in itself. Every tool represents an animal, bird, retile, or fish. Hanging from the extended roof are wind chimes made of seashells and handmade beads. All of the ornamentation gives the lodge an enchanting appearance.

No one speaks as they walk toward the totem pole. Ansel and Tom walk with reverence because they know the sacredness of this place. They do not stop at the totem pole, as the others do, but keep walking toward the lodge, where they stop and stand on the porch to watch what their students will do.

When Trudy reaches the totem pole, she brushes the tips of her fingers ever so slightly over the nose of the bison. "This looks so real!" she whispers in surprise.

The others nod in agreement; each walks around the totem pole, moving slowly, as if moving too quickly might wake the animals up. Their hands pet the bison as they move around it.

Tom and Ansel stand on the lodge porch and watch like proud parents as their group honors the animals with their respectful movements. Then Tom walks over to the entrance and starts to lift the corner of the blanket. "Should we go in now?"

"In a moment. Let's give them some more time to explore before we talk to the shaman." But as Ansel is saying these words, they feel a small breeze. The wind chimes begin to make a tinkling sound that accompanies the surrounding flute music perfectly. Both elves look to the direction of the breeze and see that it is coming from the entryway. A swirl of air makes the bottom of the blanket start to rustle, and then it moves outward and slowly creeps up until it is standing straight out. There in the opening is the shaman. He is noble in his stance and stands about five feet tall. He is thin, with dark red-brown skin, and he has a long, heavy braid of pitch-black hair. He steps forward but says nothing. His movements are more masculine than feminine, but there are no distinctive male or female features. Wearing only a long, flowing white garment, the shaman walks toward the elves and raises his hands to indicate a welcome. His voice is easy on the ears— melodious—and its pitch is in harmony with all earthly sounds.

"Peace to you! I have looked forward to your arrival!"

Tom and Ansel lower their heads slightly in a show of respect as the shaman touches their foreheads in greeting. His touch is emotional. It makes them feel even more connected to the earth and the universe beyond.

When Trudy and her friends hear the wind chimes and feel the breeze, they turn in the direction of the lodge and watch as the shaman greets the elves. They are entranced by the changing features of the being in white. The facial features change constantly from one type of forest animal to another, yet at the same time, the shaman always looks completely human. It is odd but pleasing and not scary at all. It is comforting in a way that is not understandable to any of them. It is a human face that looks like a wolf but then quickly changes and looks like an owl; then it switches again and looks like a new animal. He changes constantly, not changing at all. It is so much more than magical, subtle in its nature. They do not know what to make of this miraculous being; they stand and stare in awe. A strong love force emanates from the shaman that they can all feel. It is motherly, fatherly, and earthly. The gender of this being is not important to anyone standing there, because the being's constantly changing features capture the inquisitor's imagination, not its gender category. It is an unexplainable happening.

Trudy has to fight the urge to run up to the shaman and hug him. The force of love is strong and inviting. She looks around at the others and sees by their stares that they are feeling the same way.

The shaman turns his open arms toward the visitors as he lovingly speaks to them. "You are always safe here." His face is changing again and again as he talks. "You may come to me if you wish."

His words sound foreign to their ears even though they understand him perfectly. Trudy walks toward the shaman and puts her arms around him—or is it her? She can't tell. When they hug, Trudy feels that she has known this soul forever. The others hug the shaman too, and it seems that they all feel a loving connection to the mysterious being.

18

After greeting everyone, the shaman directs them to a clearing next to the cabin, where there is a large circle of logs that surround a small fire blazing in its center. The flame does not look as if it is burning anything; it just is. Trudy is sure that the clearing was not there before she hugged the shaman. It is all very peculiar. Everyone understands that they are being invited to sit around the fire, so they all enter the clearing and choose logs to sit upon. They are surprised as they sit down that the logs feel quite comfortable, soft as pillows. Doni rushes to sit on the log to the shaman's right side, and Trudy takes the seat on the shaman's left.

Ansel waits until everyone is seated before he makes his introduction.

"This is the most powerful shaman, the One Who Walks with the All." The shaman is still standing as he smiles first to the elf and then to the rest of them. He looks kind and gentle as his face changes from an eagle to a buffalo and then to a bear. Everyone is mesmerized by his changing features. Doni then stands up and, in an innocent voice, asks, "Are you a man or a woman?"

"I am the face of the earth. I am a reflection of everything living upon the earth." His face changes from a cougar to a pine tree and then to a tiger lily.

His answer is confusing, so Doni changes his question. "What do I call you?"

The shaman puts his hand upon Doni's head as he speaks. "You may call me what you wish, dear one. I am the beauty of the earth, the ever-changing seasons, the stillness of the Arctic, the warmth of the sun, the smell of the rain, the grass beneath your feet. I am nature."

Doni is totally charmed by the shaman. He wants to give the shaman a great name that feels good to him, and he wants the name to give honor to the shaman as well.

"Then I will call you Mother!" Doni says proudly, thinking that this is the best name of all.

The shaman looks around at the faces of the others and can see that they think this is a silly name, so he addresses them as he puts his arm around Doni's shoulders. "Mother is a good name. I have some that call me Mother Earth or Mother Nature. Others have called me Mariah, Merlin, Aine, Ashtar, Artemis, Dianna, and Melchizedek." The shaman looks at each face as he talks, and he watches how their appearances change from embarrassment to interest. "The Native Americans have many beautiful names for me, as do the ancient tribes of Africa, Australia, Mexico, and South America. I have many names. I walk with All.

"I have the universal energy and can invoke it if the people of Earth work with me. I am the one who inspires those who care for the earth and all of its inhabitants, but I am not the earth, just her companion. There are those that believe they know all truth and are in conflict with me because there are only half truths on this earth plane. They do not understand that what you believe is what you are. Most believe that they are small and cannot accomplish big ideas, but they are not small—only their thoughts are small. Humans are big and can do so much more than they choose to. Each one of you is very powerful. Your personal magic gives you more power than you can imagine." The shaman's face is changing even faster now. "I will inspire all of you to release your power and use it for good upon our planet, but as always, it will be your decision on how you will use it."

Trudy notices that her angel's orb is starting to appear over the shaman's right shoulder, just above Doni's head. As she is about to mention the appearance, Richie raises his hand to speak.

"The One Who Walks with the All?" Richie stands when he speaks.

"Yes, young one?" the shaman answers.

"If you are the most powerful shaman, why can't you accomplish the earth's care alone? Why do the people need to work with you?" Richie then sits down to listen.

"Because, dear one, the earth thrives in love, and love does not flourish alone. Love does not grow by itself. It grows when we have things to love, like each other and all of Earth's inhabitants. We show and feel love through caring for ourselves and others in the way that we live from day to day. Our devotion to the care of our surroundings is important to all of Earth's residents, because it creates love and fuels our core. The old ones, the ancients, believed in honoring everything: the ground that was walked on, their food, and what they saw, touched, heard, and felt. This honoring was good and true. It is unfortunate that this honoring has been pushed aside to make way for new thinking. New thinking and the old beliefs could have been combined if fear had not driven us apart. Fear of losing what we love is the cause of the cycle of fear we now have to contend with. Somehow we've turned to fear to protect the beings and the things that we love."

The shaman sits back down to continue his teaching. "We are born loving the self, and then we learn to love others because it gives us a wonderful feeling; it fills us with pleasure. When we think about losing the people and things that we love, fear starts to creep into our lives. We want to keep them safe, so we choose to do what we feel will accomplish this goal. Most of these acts are not the ultimate cause of fear; however, they can become a foundation for fear. As earthlings, we are vulnerable to these acts of fear. We know that we need to protect each other, but instead of it becoming an act of love, it changes into an act of fear—fear of losing the people and things that we love. The unpredictability of Earth and the elements, along with the unpredictability of all of her inhabitants, exposes us to this fear. We become weak in our love, and we try to control things that are not controllable. We should lean on each other during these times, show our love, comfort one another, protect each other, and know that there are some things that we cannot control. We need each other in order to preserve our earth and our loved ones. No one can do it alone. My energy grows when love grows—that is how my magic works. The more fear in the world, the less magic I have to offer. The smallest act of fear affects us all. This is because we are all one in the universe, and until this is accepted, fear will continue to grow. Do you understand?" The shaman then looks at all of them in turn; he is waiting for one of them to speak.

Adele has been intently listening to everything the shaman has said, and she feels that she understands, but she does not agree with him. She raises her hand. The shaman acknowledges her by his smile, and then he nods. Adele stands and looks around at the group; everyone seems interested in her query. But it is not a query at all. It is a statement that she feels strongly about.

"I don't agree with you. I think that anything done to protect the ones you love can only be done in love. I believe that if someone steps in to help another who is acting out in fear, it changes the outcome—it becomes love."

"We are of the same opinion," says the shaman. "But what if you are doing it because you feel that you can control the outcome?"

"I don't understand."

"What if you are standing up for what is right because you think it will bring you love or honor or prestige in some way—aren't you trying to control the outcome if you are not doing it strictly out of an act of love? If you do not receive the love, honor, or prestige that you want, how do you feel? Do you fear that you are not loved? Do you fear that the act was not honorable? Do you fear that it will not bring you prestige? On the other hand, if you are doing it as an act of love, you will not be expecting anything in return. You know that you are already loved, and that love is the gift to both the doer and the receiver. The act is enough.

"You are born with all the power you need; babies are very powerful— just watch them and you will see. They cannot communicate with words, yet they get what they both want and need. Of course, I am speaking of the child that is born into a family that wants them. Others grow strong in heart through trial and error on their own. It is a tough road but a rewarding road. Now, don't confuse power with control. Children learn to get what they need through love, so love is the greatest gift. As they get older, they too will act out of love, unless they have been taught another way."

The shaman chooses his words carefully; he does not want his students to misunderstand what he is trying to teach them. He lowers his voice just a bit to stress the importance of what he wants them to hear. "It seems that humans now feel that they need many things to be loved and that they must give out many things to receive love; these ideas have made way for the negative notions of greed and self-importance. Humans are willing to sacrifice the earth for their twisted philosophy of love and the perception that they can control Mother Earth and all of her creatures, and this is not true. They tear up the earth to give their loved ones the things that they assume they need and call it love, but it is really fear in disguise— fear that if they do not get these things, their loved one will cease loving them. They become greedy for these things that they believe are bringing them love; their loved ones are believing that they are more important than other creatures of the earth because they have received so many things. In fear, each one puts the blame of the earth's suffering on others instead of taking personal responsibility. You can only control the self and give love to others; you cannot expect others to love you. It is the giving of love that is all important. All actions must contain love. Love is not conditional. It is always. It is the illusion of control for love that is causing the destruction of Earth. It is this illusion that has the fairy world in such despair. This false impression has become the norm for many of the people that could have helped. It is very hard to watch the ruin of our lovely planet. That is why I only venture out on rare occasions."

The shaman points to the elves and then back to himself. "We've been watching and waiting for the thoughts of humans to change, but it is not happening. Things are getting worse. There are some small groups working in love alone; however, the larger community is still not working in love. They are starting to understand that things need to be done now, except they are doing it for the prestige or notoriety. It is all very self-indulgent. It is the want for personal attention that is slowing down their progress." The shaman's eyes fill with tears as he says these things. His sincerity and sensitivity overwhelm everyone.

Trudy wonders if all of her friends understand the immediacy and the magnitude of what the shaman is saying. She notices that her angel is still looking at her, and her loving eyes make Trudy feel safe and secure in the knowledge that she and her friends can help the earth to recover.

The shaman continues. "We need to stop blaming and to take responsibility for what is happening and love the world around us. Some have learned to do this individually, but it is imperative that we learn to do this together. This is what we must teach; we must be as one and work as the vine and the branches that one of the great masters talked about. Each one of the ascended masters taught their followers to care first for themselves and then to care for each other, working as one body. In doing so, we can take care of ourselves, our loved ones, and our home, the earth."

Adele stares deeply into the eyes of the shaman when she speaks. "How do you teach love?"

The shaman smiles at her before answering. "First, you must love and accept the self. Many search for love and can never find it. The reason that they cannot find it is because they do not know what it is. To learn love, you must first love yourself so that you can recognize it in others. Love the self first, and then the love of others will come easily. Love everyone you know, and then venture out and love all. Love always returns—maybe not in the way that you expect, but it will come back to you."

"How do you mean?" Adele questions.

"If you feel that your love is rejected by another, it is not wasted, as some think. Love is alive and will go to another who wants it. It will come back to you through another, or maybe through a pet or your work or your creativity. It always comes back—that is why you must try to be open to All, so that you do not reject love by your actions."

Jeff is not taking any of this lightly. "Do you mean that we should love everyone? Even people that are bad?"

The shaman stands again, walks over to Jeff, puts his hands gently on his shoulders, and talks directly to him. "I know that some of you have suffered at the hands of terrible people, but I am not speaking of good or bad." Then he turns and continues to talk to everyone as he moves around the circle. "There are many souls upon the earth that do not know love. They are mean and think only of the self. There are many complicated reasons for this; however, each reason breaks down into the fact that their soul does not know love. The first group only considers their earthly pursuits and can only love themselves, and the second group loves nothing, not even the self they blind themselves to others. Both groups despise themselves and have no respect for the self; therefore, they cannot show love or respect for others—they hurt themselves and others. They move about their lives destroying others because they do not see their own self-worth, which makes them worthless. Some do this in all ways because they have no conscience; they can hurt and take life from those that love them. A conscience grows only with love; if there is no love present, then there is no conscience. Love gives one the desire to go beyond the self to give and receive love. But know that there are those who give the impression of love by taking care of themselves, the people around them, and the area in which they live. They are only doing it to make themselves happy; they see the people in their lives as possessions and not as loved ones. They do not recognize the love of others, but they want to look right to the world around them. They do not feel love; they do not know what love is. If they lose a person or possession, they just replace it. They may feel the loss but do not suffer the loss of love. This, of course, hurts those around them, but the executor will not feel it; they will not understand it, and they do not recognize the love of others. The truth is that if you love yourself, you will not hurt yourself or others; this works in all ways. If you love the earth, you will not hurt it or its inhabitants."

"But we all hurt each other sometimes," says Jeff, "whether we mean to or not. Does that mean that we weren't taught to love right?"

"No. It means that we are of the earth and make mistakes and bad choices now and then, but it is not a way of life. Hopefully, you do not live this way all of the time. If you have the intention to love, then most of the things that you do will turn out in love, even though it may not seem that way all of the time. Because we are all different, we see things differently, and that can be a problem at times, but if we try to live our lives in love, then we can get through our problems and share our disappointments with others and respect our differences. We learn from mistakes and bad choices, and what we learn is usually for the good of All.

"We know that you all love each other, and that is a great beginning. What we want you to do is recognize the love in yourself and in your companions—to truly feel it and then teach it to others around you through your loving feelings and actions. Help spread love into your community and out into the world in general. These actions will bring you the power you need to attract those who will listen, because that is how the universe works. See love in all things and love will come to you. Mother Earth loves you, and you are drawn to her because you are love, and she needs your power to help empower her. In so doing, she can repair the damage that has been done to her. Earth's inhabitants need to see her as love and not as a problem. Problems are negative thoughts. She needs positive, loving thoughts and actions.

"There will be many who will think that these actions are ridiculous, but you can use the mighty force of love with them also. Surround these people with love, and accept them for who they are and move on. Some will see the sense in what you are doing; others will not. Do not let the thoughts of others pull you down. Their way of thinking is negative, and their behavior is negative too."

Doni raises his hand, and the shaman acknowledges him by nodding toward the boy. Doni stands respectfully and quietly says, "Are you saying that all we have to do is use our hearts and show love? Don't we have to really do anything?"

"I am saying, young one, that you must use love in all of your actions. If you have decided that you will help Mother Nature by keeping her clean, then every time that you see a piece of paper on the ground or a plastic bag stuck in a bush or a dog pile in the park, you clean it up with a gratitude of love and not disgust or dislike for a fellow inhabitant. Your point of view is very important when you are trying to complete an action of love. Mother Earth can sense your feelings, and she loves all of her family; she does not judge, as we do."

"But what about those people who don't care? Should we clean up after them?" Cori is upset at the thought that others will use her to do their work. "Shouldn't they be taught to clean up after themselves? Wouldn't they just be using us because they know that they can? How is that good for the earth?"

"You have many good questions, and I will do my best to answer them in the way of the Mother. To love is the most important thing we can ever learn to do. The journey to love would seem easy; however, it is a most complicated path. There is no end to this journey—no finish line and no easy conclusion. There will always be stumbling blocks in your way because love grows; it is not motionless. The more you love, the more love will ask of you and the more love you will receive. Every one of us is different, so there will never be one way to love; there will never be one way of showing it. There are as many ways to love as there are beings on this planet. When you come across someone that does not know love, the only thing you can do is show love—wrap yourself in it and deliver it to them, and then if they do not understand, it is best to move on. When you are cleaning up for someone else, do not see it as doing their job; instead, see it as showing Mother Earth how much you love her. Be positive, not negative. They will see your love of the earth, and then it becomes their responsibility to show love or not; it is always a free choice, and the choice may not be easy. By doing this act, you are teaching, and that is what we are asking you to do.

"An important factor to remember is that love is not something that is given or received only once. It grows and changes just like everything else on this planet. It must be nurtured in order to grow, and it is more than words. It is more than a look, a kiss, a hug, or a good deed. Love is our power to change and to grow, and it must be embraced and held on to. It is a true energy that everyone is born with, but not everyone knows how to find it and use it. It is a force that must be released in order for it to be effective. You must understand this; you all have this ability, and you all have the authority to use it to its highest potential. Our hope is that this is exactly what you will choose to do."

Trudy keeps her eye on her angel as the shaman talks, and she notices that the orb begins to grow during these last few words. She also senses that the others can now see her and feel her presence. Trudy is amazed when, without turning in the direction of the orb, the shaman raises a hand and invites the angel to join the circle.

"Come and sit with us, angel of love and light," he says.

To Trudy's surprise, and to the astonishment of the others, Danielle walks out of the orb. She is transparent and is wearing a soft-textured golden gown that flows gently around her as she walks. She is tall, maybe seven feet, but extremely delicate. Her wings are white with rainbow-colored tips, and her brown hair is long past her shoulders. It moves as if it has a life all of its own. Her face is kind and gentle, with no color, and is ageless in appearance. She floats directly to Trudy and then kneels down to embrace her. The love that radiates from her is so pure that it causes Trudy to shudder. Trudy puts her arms around Danielle, but she can barely feel anything solid as she tries to hug back. The angel then greets each person and elf in the same way; the love that emanates from her is strong and heartfelt in a way that no one is expecting. She stops in front of the shaman, and smiling, the two of them embrace. Sparks shoot out from both of them and ignite a rainbow of pastel colors that begin swirling around them; it is a glorious sight. A wonderful aroma bursts from the two of them and permeates the air with the smell of freshly baked cookies, or maybe it is cake or pies or the smell of the best bakery on Earth. The entire group is smiling; they all feel extremely joyful! The sight injects a power into their souls. They all feel that they can accomplish anything asked of them. At this moment, they understand their inherent magic and their power, even if they cannot yet verbalize it.

They all join hands and encircle the shaman and the angel; it is the happiest moment of their lives together. Each one gaily laughs in pure ecstasy as sparks of pastel color shoot out from them, making a swirling rainbow as they move. Trudy notices that their feet have left the ground and that they are moving slowly upward as they dance. Around and around in this miraculous dance of love they go, happy to be together and happy to be! Trudy notices something else as they all move in this incredible dance; other angels are appearing around them. It seems as if hundreds of them have joined in the merriment. When Trudy makes eye contact with any of them, she feels a shot of love that boosts her feelings of joy to a higher level. It is incomparably exhilarating!

The dance has come to an end; however, they all feel as if they are still moving, because their hearts are full and beating quickly. The thrill of what just happened is more than anyone could have expected. The group is now seated around the fire; the guardian angels of each of them are now present and visible. All of them are appreciating the joyous experience of just being together and communicating without words. They are experiencing the love of the force that draws them all together. Feeling their connection to one another makes them realize that there is no real separation of spirit from one to another and that each person is important because they are all one.

While everyone is taking pleasure in the moment, a beautiful red spark grows out of the fire. As it grows, a feminine figure emerges and seems to stand tall upon it. Her hair is dark as night and lovingly weaved with lotus flowers, and she wears a stunning red Asian gown that falls past her feet. The gown is exquisitely embroidered with gold threads. When everyone's attention is drawn to her, she begins to speak with a most pleasing Asian accent. "I am Kwan Yin, ascended master. I am here because I value your power, and I am pleased that you will be taking on such a heartfelt project. Honor yourself, and know the significance of your power. Enjoy the process upon which you embark. Do not chide yourself or others for mistakes; learn and grow from them. Love, love,

love! You may call upon me at any time to comfort and protect you. Look for me inside every flower. My spirit is with you always." She then vanishes in a puff of red smoke.

"Who was that?" Jeff then rephrases his question, knowing that she said her name. "I mean, who is Kwan Yin, and what is an ascended master?"

The shaman stands to answer and addresses all who are there in a humble voice. "You have a book in the outer world that I will quote from to answer your question; it is called *A Course in Miracles Manual for Teachers*. There are those who have reached God directly, retaining no trace of worldly limits and remembering their own identity perfectly. These might be called the teachers of teachers, because although they're no longer visible, their image can yet be called upon. And they will appear when and where it's helpful for them to do so. To those for whom such appearances would be frightening, they give their ideas. No one can call on them in vain. Nor is there anyone of whom they're unaware. All needs are known to them, and all mistakes are recognized and overlooked by them. The time will come when this is understood. And meanwhile, they give all their gifts to the teachers of God who look to them for help."

Then the shaman asks, "Do you understand what these words mean?"

"Yes!" Trudy rises to her feet. "The words mean that the woman was a heavenly visitor and that she can really help us if we ask. And that we will learn from her even if we can't see her. She won't judge us by our mistakes, because they are all overlooked by heavenly beings." Trudy is proud of her answer, and it shows in her face as she sits back down.

The shaman smiles at her as his face changes from an otter to an eagle. "You understand much for one so young. There are many masters that you can call upon for help. You will learn who they are as you continue this journey. It will be very exciting for all of you. You will gain much power. You will start with your own households and move on to your community, city, state, and country, and before you know it, you will be learning and teaching about our global community and how we all can share in taking care of Mother Earth. This is your mission: teach the world to love themselves and Mother Earth while loving and honoring yourself and valuing your power. Do not get angry at yourself or others for mistakes, but learn and grow from them. Never judge. Do not give up hope. Learn to laugh at your mistakes, and in your laughter, always show love for yourself and others. Some will see you as liars, but most will understand your words. Some will come to your aid, and some will want to watch and see what happens. But those that you inspire will be many. They will step up to help if their mission is clear and understood. Work together and you will succeed; harmony is the key. And always make time to have fun!"

"But what if we are afraid to do this?" asks Melissa. "What if we can't do what you ask of us?"

"Observe the tiny caterpillar. It came into this beautiful world not knowing what to do, but it knows that it is very hungry to get on with its mission in life. It digests many things, not knowing why, on its slow journey of change. Moving forward, it must dodge many enemies and pitfalls before it can change, but it does change. Unafraid, it continues, and little by little, it learns what it must do and gradually adheres to the idea of change as it enters the protection of the chrysalis to adjust to all that it has learned. In doing so, it becomes something new and beautiful. The butterfly shows us that you can move from one kind of life to another without fear as long as you take your time and know that Earth Mother will always protect you. Once you have had time to digest all that you have learned, you will be able to transform yourselves and others without fear, even if you do not say one word. Your life will show your beliefs. You will have changed into a beautiful butterfly, and everyone will be able to see it whether they acknowledge you or not. This is how you will teach. Do not be afraid.

"Peace be with you." The shaman starts to rise above the ground; sparks of gold emanate from his being. "Enjoy the work in which you now embark. The world needs you!"

In a twinkling, the shaman and the angels disappear; some golden flakes drift down around the area where the fire once burned. The fire is gone, and all is quiet. All that remains are Ansel, Tom, Trudy, and her friends. Even the logs have disappeared. Everyone looks toward Ansel for some kind of explanation for the magical disappearance of the shaman and the angels, but there is none to give. Silence invades the area as they stare at one another. They are each proud that they have been chosen to do this work, but they are also questioning their capabilities at the same time.

"You will become more confident as you begin to take action," says Ansel, as if he knows what they are all thinking. "The hardest step is always the first one, and as soon as you take it, you will begin to grow more convinced that you are doing the right thing."

"Well, let's take that step," says Tom as he gives a wave.

Richie and Jeff start to follow the elves out of the area, and slowly, the others trail behind them. No one speaks, but all are still feeling the joy of what has happened.

The group follows the elves out of the surrounding area and down a well-worn path for what seems a long distance before anyone speaks.

Cori is holding Ansel's hand as they walk. He is almost her height, so she can look him in the eyes as she questions him. "Where are we going, Ansel?" She isn't tired or bored; she is curious.

"We are taking you to see the wise ones of the animal kingdom. They will also inspire you and make your magic stronger."

Doni runs up beside them. "Are they shamans too?"

"Well, yes. In a way, they are. However, we don't usually refer to animals as shamans; we call them wise ones."

"Do they live in a lodge?" Doni is excited to meet with these animals.

"No. They live out in nature, as all animals do."

The others are now coming in closer to listen in on this conversation.

Cori is also eager to meet these wise ones. "What kind of animals are they?"

Ansel slows down just a bit so that everyone can hear his answer. "Our hope is to meet with the great rabbit Manabozho, whose wondrous deeds are many, and Tatanka, the white buffalo, who is the sacred symbol of life and abundance to the outer world of North America."

The trail that they are following has widened enough that they can all walk side by side. The grasses surrounding them have turned a soft brown color, and large cactus plants with beautiful blooms atop most of them are everywhere. The ground they are walking upon has changed from a dark, muddy brown to a dusty reddish purple. There are giant red rocks jutting out from the land. In the distance, they can see snow-capped mountains in a panoramic view that seemingly goes on forever. The sky is a brilliant blue, and there are no clouds; just the vague outline of the moon is visible.

"This place we are walking into looks like the pictures I've seen of the Southwest," says Adele.

"Yes," comments Ansel, "it does resemble the outer world of your southwestern states. The animals that live here desire an aired area that looks like your West."

"Did the great rabbit and the white buffalo ever live in the outer world?" asks Melissa.

"No," says Tom, who is walking next to her, "they never actually lived in the outer world; they just visited their brothers and sisters who lived there. They still visit on occasion."

"Do they bite?" Melissa whispers to Tom. She doesn't want the others to know that she is worried about that.

"They do have teeth," Tom whispers back with a smile, "but I've never heard of either of them biting anyone."

Melissa lets out a small sigh of relief. "That's good."

Doni stops and points to a dust cloud in the distance. "Look at that brown cloud. What is it?"

A large brown cloud is forming over the plains' grasses. It seems miles away, but it is suddenly upon them, and everyone can see it.

"It's a herd of horses!" yells Trudy.

Ansel and Tom gently push everyone to the side of the pathway and have them all stand next to a huge red rock for protection as the wild horses pass them by. They are fine-looking animals; each one looks as if it is getting ready to take off and fly into the air. It is a spectacular sight! The dust stays up high enough that it doesn't bother any of the spectators. Everyone can see and breathe perfectly. They are all smiling as the horses pass. They expect a loud galloping sound, but there is only a soft pounding sound that is musical, like all of the sounds in the inner world. The sound gives a bass tone that harmonizes with the flute and drum they have been listening to.

"Awesome!" yell the twins. They are hugging each other and jumping up and down with the joy that only a child can express.

"They are the most beautiful horses I've ever seen!" squeaks Melissa.

Then, suddenly, they hear a deep, smooth-toned voice: "They are our brothers and sisters."

Everyone turns and looks to where the voice is coming from, and in the settling dust, they can see an enormous white beast. At first, the sight is startling, but as the dust settles, they can see the sensitive brown eyes of the radiant white bison that stands before them. The animal is immense but not frightening, and it looks as if it is smiling at them. As the final particles of dust settle, they also notice an extremely large hare standing next to the bison. The rabbit has reddish-brown fur and gigantic ears that stand straight up. This animal also looks as if it is happy. Its wise, large, perceptive brown eyes staring back at the group have just an air of caution in them.

Tom steps forward and speaks with great enthusiasm to the pair. "Great ones," he says with his arms outstretched, "we have brought people from the outer world to see and talk with you." He steps back and bows.

Ansel puts his hand out toward the visitors and introduces them. "This is Trudy, Jeff, Richie, Doni, Melissa, and Cori. I am Ansel, and this is Tom." Then, switching hands and bowing toward the hare, he says, "This is Manabozho, whose wondrous deeds are many." The rabbit's ears twitch just a bit, and his head bows. Ansel then takes a small step forward and points to the white bison. "And this is Lila Wakan, the white buffalo. She brings us the messages of the great mystery, our reasons for being." As Ansel speaks, a white fog rises from the ground and slowly covers the bison. The fog begins to take on the shape of a woman while soaking up the shape of the white buffalo and making it disappear. Then out of the heavy mist walks a delicate-looking beauty. She is dressed completely in white, with her long blue-black hair hanging loose except for one small braid on her left side. It is tied with a strip of buffalo fur. Her eyes are dark and imposing with great power, and above each cheek is a small red painted dot. Her kind face is extraordinary in that it projects an air of knowing All. Each person looking into her eyes feels that she knows him or her through and through. There is no need for an introduction.

Trudy and the others are completely stunned by what they see, and they know that they are in the presence of a glorious being. Trudy also notices that when Lila Wakan moves toward them, her feet do not touch the ground. Her feet don't move at all; she just glides toward them.

Manabozho sits still; his ears move only slightly when someone speaks. He is a magnificent animal, regal in stature and gentle in appearance.

"Welcome, human beings!" Lila Wakan's voice is deep, smooth, and dreamy sounding. "Please sit and hear my words." She points at an area behind them. When they turn to look, they are surprised to see a huge willow tree surrounded by a carpet of green grass and many wildflowers; after all, they are in the desert of the Southwest. How can this be? They are also surprised to see Manabozho sitting under the willow tree. Trudy quickly looks back to where she last saw him, but of course he is gone.

"Wow!" yelps Doni as he stares at the hare. "How'd you do that?"

"Manabozho is quiet," explains Ansel, "but he holds great magic."

Manabozho sits in silence as the group gets comfortable. They all keep an eye on him as they sit down, just in case he moves again. They want to see his magic with their own eyes.

"Beautiful beings," the melodious voice of Lila Wakan begins. "I can see that you have already learned much on your visit here. You are all very respectful to our presence, and I am proud to know you and pleased to be your teacher." She moves in closer to her students and sits with them; she floats cross-legged just above the ground. "The shaman has given you your mission, and we will help you to understand it so that you will not waver in your abilities.

"The entire universe works in love, not just Earth Mother, and that is why the shaman told you to love yourself first. When you love yourself, only words of love will you use. Loving words cause loving actions. The words you speak can carry harmony or discord to others. Words are very powerful and can hurt and destroy if not used in love, so it is important to know how words work. Your words come to you through the power of thought. You use energy to think. It is this energy that carries your power—the power to give out love to others and to the earth. You have the magical power to create a thought that can change the world! This energy is true magic! You can use this energy for good or for evil; all beings have this power just as we do, but most do not understand it. You have a choice on how you will use this power, for good or for bad, or you may choose not to use it at all, but it is always freedom of choice. No one can choose for you, because it is your power. The power of your thoughts equals the power of your love. This love goes out to others in thoughts and also in deeds. This is love in action!" As Lila Wakan talks, her hands and body move in a way that draws the listeners to her; she is strong yet gentle. Her every movement has meaning, and every facial expression shows power and concern. Even the softness of her hair moves in love.

"When you think and act in love at all times, then you are using your power to create a better world." Lila looks closely at all of them. "These are not empty words." A tear drops from one of her beautiful brown eyes. "Your world has used these words many times without true meaning behind them, so they have lost much of their power in the minds of your people. These words are true. You must believe them. Love will create a better world if put into right action."

Trudy is deeply moved by the words of Lila Wakan, and she really wants to comply with all that Lila asks of them. "How do we put love into action?" she asks.

"You, my dear Trudy, and your beautiful friends here do this every day in small ways, which is good. You do it without even noticing, which is very good. You do it by picking up an empty can someone has haphazardly tossed to the ground or by cleaning up some candy wrappers that have carelessly been dropped. These actions show respect, love, and gratitude to Mother Earth. You also do it when you are saying kind words to each other, making someone laugh, or helping out your families and friends in various ways. This shows your love to mankind. All of this is great and good, but we are asking more of you, my children. Teach people to do more. Our beautiful world is in crisis because your outer world is not being taken care of. You must take action immediately, or both of our worlds will crumble. Some will say that it is too late to change things, but it is not." Lila Wakan becomes silent for a moment in order to allow them to absorb her words.

"You must teach your world to care for their mother, Mother Earth. This caring goes out much further than caring for family and friends. Make them understand that every living thing is important in keeping the earth healthy. Every animal, every bird, every fish, every tree and plant, every drop of water is your brother or your sister. This is what we ask of you. This is what you must do! Use your power to change the world!" She again stops for a moment to let the words sink in. Then, standing, she swings her arms out. "Look around our inner world, and tell me what you notice that is different in the way that things are."

Melissa quickly answers. "You have dragons and fairies here."

"That is true; however, at one time, they were in both worlds. What do you need in your world in order for them to want to come back?"

Richie stands up to address the entire group, but he looks directly at Lila Wakan and then quickly at his notes before speaking. "You said before that harmony is what works, and I've noticed that everything here works in harmony. I believe that is why we constantly hear music. The music is not from a single source, and it is not from instruments; it is, in fact, coming from all things working together. Everything here makes a sound that comes from being happy—that is the source of the music. Things are happy here because All is treasured by every other thing. You are all gentle here; even the dragon was gentle, and as her wings fluttered, they played a slight musical sound. Your world is different because it works in harmony, in love, with all things."

Lila Wakan is smiling as Richie gives his theory. "Yes. Yes! That is it! That is very true. There is much discord in the outer world. You have so much noise that you cannot hear or feel any of the harmony that is there. The power of love brings harmony to all things. Love is the quiet divine force that moves all things in the universe. It is not loud and noisy, but gentle and kind."

"But we do show love!" Adele breaks in. "We love our parents, and they love us."

Cori takes Adele's hand as she stands and cries out, "And we love our friends and our pets and where we live, too!"

"And each other," Doni says as he stands by his brother and Jeff.

Lila Wakan smiles at all of them in such a loving way that they all sit back down to listen to her. "That is all true. Your love is very big, and that is why we need you. You must go out and find others like yourselves who are not afraid to show love in big ways. You must always use your thoughts in loving ways as you search for them. Your thoughts create vibrations from your soul, and these vibrations can be felt by others. It is the high vibrations of your loving thoughts that can change the world. Your vibrations will reverberate in others, and this will help you to find them. Then as you teach them and their vibrations become stronger, they will reach out until all have reached a harmonious vibration of love. This is truly how love works. This is the magic that we all possess. Unfortunately, the opposite of love is fear, and fear works in the same way. Fear is your biggest enemy because people can disguise it for themselves by believing that it is love."

"How does that happen?" Jeff interrupts. "How can fear be love?"

"Fear is not love. Fear is the opposite of love. Humans confuse this often, thinking that hate is the opposite of love, but hate is created from fear. Love is freedom, and fear is oppression. Fear is formed from a belief that one can control outside of the self. You can only control your thoughts and your actions; no one can control the thoughts and actions of others. Love and right action are what will heal the world; Mother Earth can feel your love, and that is what she thrives upon.

"When one thinks he or she has control over someone else's actions, situations, or thoughts is when fear steps in and takes over. It starts in such a seemingly good way. Many feel that if they can somehow control all situations, nothing bad will ever happen to them or to those they love. But this is a fear thought that causes fear actions; it is not a love thought. Guidance is a love thought and action. Information is a love action. Freedom of choice is a love action.

"When people are young, they need to learn; they need information, guidance, and choices. One learns by cause and effect. If individuals do not have these things when young, they will not make good choices when grown up. This is the difference between those whose love is free and those whose love is based in fear. This difference is important because it means that one person is learning in fear, while the other is making choices and learning by cause and effect. In the hurry-up world that you live in, children are not all given the time to learn in this way. Adults feel pressure in keeping their children safe, but instead of taking the time to teach them, their fear for the child's safety causes them to shelter their offspring. In this way, the child is not free to learn and becomes fearful instead. These humans are looked at by their children as authoritarian in their attitudes because they are forcing their children to do as they say instead of learning with guidance and cause and effect. This does not teach love and respect. There is no one who is singularly at fault here; it is a problem that has developed over time, and it must change. Love is giving each soul time to learn with information, guidance, and choice. Fear is fooling these well-meaning humans into believing that they are acting out of love, but it is fear, not love.

"The entire planet works in this way. People may feel fear in the need to provide everything to their family, their country, and the world. The fear that they will not have enough has caused many problems for the earth. Fear brings on manipulation by some leaders and the victimization of some of their followers. Fear that bad things will happen to loved ones has caused much of this. There are times when bad things will happen, but fear will not help the situation. You have seen many incidents where bad things have happened to those with much abundance and plenty of protection, so you can see that having many things will not stop the lessons of the soul. We are here on this planet to learn, to grow, to love, to give, and to forgive. It is in our best interest to give out as much love as we can and to teach others to do the same."

Adele has trouble keeping herself calm while Lila Wakan speaks; she does not agree with what she is hearing. "Parents who *do* love their children tell them what to do for their own protection. They are protecting their kids from all the bad stuff that can happen to them!"

Lila Wakan glides over to Adele, puts her hand upon her shoulder in a loving caress, and looks her straight in the eye. With a soft, loving voice, she says, "Is it not a greater gift to take the time to explain and teach your children and to give them the guidance to seek an opportunity to learn on their own? This is love. This is the same gift that the Mighty Spirit gives to all of us. It is freedom of choice. I am not saying that you should not care for your child or others, because that would be unwise. I am saying that we need to think and act with love and not fear when caring for them. We should all have the freedom to choose our own path in this lifetime. Do you now see the importance of learning all of our choices through cause and effect? If we were ordered to take only one path, what would we learn? If we are told that there is only one way to be and only one path to follow, how would we be different? An artist who was told to follow the path of a football player would not find happiness, even though he knew he was loved, would he? He would not be able to show his love completely, because he would be following a path that was not of his choosing. What would make him unhappy is the inability to have a choice; he did not learn on his own if he could be a great football player or a great artist. He may have been able to do both, but because he did not have the freedom of choice, he did not have the choice to learn if he was good at both, so he will never know for sure what his calling was. This uncertainty makes one fear the future. When one has fear of the future, one cannot act out in pure love. One can love; however, it will be filled with doubt, hesitations, and insecurity, clogging up the purity of that love. We must stop this flow of fear, for it is very contagious. It sneaks up and attaches itself to your love and steals the purity away."

Then, from behind them, they hear a deep voice: "This is a great truth! This is the truth that the outer world has forgotten."

Lila looks up and smiles at the figure behind them as the others turn to see him. They are surprised to see that Manabozho has turned into a human being. He is sitting upon a gigantic white horse. He has two long white feathers hanging from his braided dark brown hair, and the dark red skin of his bare chest seems to blaze as he speaks. He appears to have a large dream catcher draped over his left arm.

"These words are true," Manabozho says. "When you love people, you must speak truth to them. All need truth for deciding correct action. They need choice for learning from wrong action as well as good. This freedom of choice with guidance is love!" Manabozho pauses for a moment and then adds, "Do not be so afraid of losing your body that you lose the mind. The mind—your soul—is who you are, not the body. Many of Earth's spiritual leaders understood this concept and tried to teach it as we do now."

As Manabozho speaks, the wind begins to churn, causing the red desert dust to rise up like a phantom and swirl around the feet of Manabozho's horse. Lila Wakan becomes transparent, and her body begins to turn slowly into smoke. The smoke rises into the air, taking her shape with it and leaving the white buffalo standing in her place. The buffalo looks into the eyes of all who are there. She then turns to look at Manabozho and nods to him; as she does this, he begins to speak again to the group.

"You have the great gift of understanding your mission. You all know of your magic. Now you must go and spread this gift to all in the outer world. Your understanding will give others strength and courage. Together you can save Mother Earth from destruction; there are many in the outer world who can help if guided in the right direction. Be alert, and look for people around you who can help. We will always be with you in spirit. If you should need us, just put us in your thoughts, and we will work with you. That is our gift to you; that is our promise."

They all watch as Manabozho and Lila Wakan leave them. The red sand at the feet of the spiritual teachers starts to swirl and then turns to smoke. The smoke drifts upward and around the two, transforming them into puffy white clouds that stand out and embellish the blue of the desert sky. The elves hold hands with the rest of the group as they stare skyward. Some of the smoke stays, penetrating the watchers' souls. The powerful feeling that they are left with stays strong in their hearts, along with the belief that they are greatly loved by All. They all understand their mission deep in their beings; it is an incredible moment that lasts less than an outer-world minute, yet it feels as though it is forever. The elves notice that each of the humans seems to shimmer with an iridescent light. They then watch the children's bodies vibrate at a high rate of speed and spew out all the colors of the rainbow. The brightest color of pink shoots out from their chests. This makes the elves excited, as they know that this colorful vibration is the vibration of love. At that instant, they all know that they will do anything in their power to succeed. They understand that they are part of the Great Spirit that rises in every human heart and mind. They understand that by changing their thoughts and actions, they will be empowered, and therefore, they will be able to change the world! They know that spirit is everywhere and in everything. Living mind is the immortal life force that is the Great Spirit! They feel the effects of the pure love that the great teachers gave them. They know and understand the powerful impact that each human being has on the environment of the outer world. They are forever changed!

Trudy sits in the cushy green grass under the huge willow tree with the fingertips of her right hand gliding in and out of the cool water of the brook next to her. She is slowly coming out of the trancelike feeling she was left with after her grand realization of the power that she holds. As she looks around at her companions, she sees that they must be feeling the same way, because each of them has a slight smile. Their faces look older, wiser, and more attractive than they were before. Trudy feels a stronger, more encompassing love for each of them. It is an extremely good feeling!

"It is time for your return."

Trudy looks toward Tom as he speaks; she notices a calmness about him that was not there before. His face looks softer somehow and not as old.

Doni stands up and rubs his eyes. "It will be a long walk back, won't it?"

"Not really," Ansel says as he reaches for the hands of Cori and Melissa. "The journey here felt like a long time; however, it truly wasn't. We took the path that we did because you needed time to think about what you've seen and heard here. It is important that you have time to process the information you were given so that you can come up with a course of action that suits you. Now that you've had this experience, the journey back will pass quickly."

Everyone stands and follows Ansel and Tom. Tom walks in front of the group, along with Ansel and the twins, while Doni, Richie, and Jeff follow behind them. Richie has his pad out and is writing about their encounter with Lila Wakan and Manabozho as they walk. Doni is quiet. Trudy and Adele are at the back of the troop. They have their arms around each other and are smiling. Everyone walks slowly, as if they have all the time in the world at their disposal.

It isn't long before they can see the grand oak tree in the distance. Their fairy friends are flying toward them, waving and happy to see them.

"Wow, you were right!" says Doni. "It took no time at all to get back."

"It's so magical here, isn't it, Tru?" Adele squeezes her friend's shoulder before letting go. "I just love it!"

"Me too!" gushes Trudy. She is happy to hear that her friend is feeling the same way.

Trudy and Adele run forward to meet their fairy friends. They can feel the love from the fairies grow as they get closer to them. The background music blends well with the sweet little hum caused by the movements of the fairies' wings. Then they all notice that they too have sounds! The sounds are caused by the vibration of the love they are feeling. The noise is the resonance, the reverberations of love! They are in harmony with All! Each one of them starts laughing as he or she realizes the synchronization of his or her personal sound. It is the best feeling ever to be part of the beautiful sounds of the earth.

The first fairy to reach them is, of course, Topsy. He flies directly to Doni, who is excited to see him. "I'm so glad that you're back!" Topsy declares. "Did you have fun?"

"It was great!" Doni gives Topsy a high five, causing the little fairy to be pushed backward a bit, and they both laugh along with everyone else.

"I'm so glad that you are back!" Orange Blossom sings out in excitement. "I want to hear everything. Everything!"

"We all do!" cries Nena as she proceeds to hug everyone she sees.

The walk back to the oak tree is fun. They are all laughing and excited as they hear the stories that the travelers tell.

During the narrative of Trudy's angel appearance, Trudy thinks she sees the tail of the fox in the bushes beside them. This makes her a bit uneasy as she relates her story of Danielle. She is not fearful, as she was before, but she is eager to find out why the fox has been following them. She cuts her story short as she runs to see this mysterious creature, but as always, it disappears before she can catch up with it.

"Hey, Tru!" yells out Richie as he chases after her. "What's going on?"

"I saw that fox again." Trudy's voice sounds disappointed as she turns to Richie. "And it disappeared again, too."

Richie puts his hand on Trudy's shoulder as he speaks, which is uncharacteristic of him. "Look, Tru, I know you feel that this fox means something to you, but maybe it's just a curious animal too shy to approach us."

Trudy shrugs Richie's hand off of her shoulder and takes it into her hand. "I know you guys think that I'm making a big deal out of nothing, but I don't agree with you. Something inside of me knows that this fox wants to follow me, not you and not them"—she points to the others—"and I want to know why. I know this seems odd, but I feel it wants to talk with me alone or something."

"Yeah, then why does it always run away when you get near it?"

"I don't know. Maybe it wants me to follow it."

"Or maybe it's just bringing you a message that you can't understand yet. You know, like maybe it's your totem and just protects you and doesn't need you to follow it."

"Whatever." Trudy is disappointed in Richie's answer. *But he may have a point.*

"Well, it's too late now, so let's catch up with everyone else." Richie pulls her toward him and starts walking back to the group. Trudy reluctantly goes along without saying another word.

The reunion is grand! Everyone is laughing and hugging as they approach the old oak tree. It seems as though everyone in the inner world is there to wish them well. They are again invited into the grand ballroom for drinks and treats as everyone celebrates their return. The king and queen are there to give them their blessings and hopes in their desire to create an environment of ease and goodwill between both worlds.

The comfortable feeling that they are all experiencing is abruptly intruded upon as some sprites enter the ballroom in a fretful state. The anxious looks on the faces of these gentle water nymphs causes the crowd to separate and give them a direct path to the royal couple. The mermaids and the mermen in the room also come forward in their desire to learn what the emergency is.

"Your Highness." The red-haired sprite speaks first as she bows her tiny head toward the queen.

The queen takes a serious stance as she speaks. "What news do you bring us, dear one?" She tries to keep her voice calm as she takes the hand of Gentle Mountain Lion. She knows that these small, delicate creatures would never interrupt a gathering like this unless this were an urgent situation.

The sprite looks around the grand ballroom before she speaks. She has a desperate look upon her face that penetrates the hearts of Trudy and her friends. When the small creature begins to talk, everyone becomes silent. "Our mother's veins have become so polluted in the outer world that some more of our dear friends are dying. We need your help right away!"

"Please calm yourself and explain." The queen and king give her their full attention as the sprite continues.

Trudy leans over to whisper to Blossom, "Whose mother is she referring to?"

"Mother Earth, darling—Gaia," Blossom whispers back. "Her veins are the waterways. Water is the blood of the earth; without it, she will die. That is one of the most important reasons we want you and your friends to help us out. Our mother's blood is being poisoned, and the outer world needs to help her. She needs the love of all of her children!"

And this, my dear reader, is where our first adventure ends and our next begins, so I shall tell you that our heroes do have an opportunity to go home and relate this first adventure to Grandma Maya, who gives them some advice and encouragement. They return to their homes and give thanks for their families and enjoy them before their return.

Thank you for being present in my spirit and hearing my mighty song. It gives me strength and the hope that I might survive and live out the life I was promised as a tiny acorn when planted and cared for by the fairies.

Remember to love and care for Gaia.

www.ingramcontent.com/pod-product-compliance
Lightning Source LLC
LaVergne TN
LVHW092049060526
838201LV00047B/1300